Faith blinked and stared into his eyes. Truth dawned. "Ray?"

"Faith?" They spoke at the same time.

He winked, and her breath caught. For a moment she went dizzy as memories flooded her mind. *Ray!* She dashed around the counter but caught herself before she jerked him into a hug. They stood face-to-face for what seemed an eternity.

"We need to catch up, but I have an emergency here." He held the dog out for her inspection.

Her attention dropped to the tiny creature. "What happened? Is she yours?"

CANDICE SPEARE lives with her husband and family, along with Jack the Dog, in Maryland. She loves to hear from her readers. You may contact her by visiting her Web site: www.candicemillerspeare.com.

NANCY TOBACK was born and raised in Manhattan and now resides in sunny Florida. Her passion for writing fiction began way back in grammar school. If there's spare time after being wife, mother, grandmother, writer, and avid reader, Nancy is a watercolorist and charcoal artist and enjoys gourmet cooking. You may e-mail her at backtonan@aol.com.

Books by Candice Speare and Nancy Toback

HEARTSONG PRESENTS
HP885—A Hero for Her Heart
HP905—Boxed into Love

Don't miss out on any of our super romances. Write to us at the following address for information on our newest releases and club information.

Heartsong Presents Readers' Service
PO Box 721
Uhrichsville, OH 44683

Or visit www.heartsongpresents.com

Mending Fences

Candice Speare and Nancy Toback

Heartsong Presents

To my dad, Walter,
for his love and encouragement all my life.
I love you.

Nancy

To Kim, my real life hero.

Candice

A note from the Authors:
We love to hear from our readers! You may correspond with us by writing:

Candice Speare and Nancy Toback
Author Relations
PO Box 721
Uhrichsville, OH 44683

ISBN 978-1-61626-064-4

MENDING FENCES

Our mission is to publish and distribute inspirational products offering exceptional value and biblical encouragement to the masses.

PRINTED IN THE U.S.A.

one

Ray Reed exited Interstate 405, turning his rental truck west toward Bothell. He drove at a sedate pace, eyeing the familiar landscape. Peace settled over him as he breathed in the rain-scented air.

Thank God he was home. He missed Bothell in the months he'd taken leave. Or as his brother Philip would say: "You ran away."

Philip was right. Ray had run away, especially from his emotions, but he'd needed a change of scenery. Now he knew without a doubt where he should be. Bothell. What remained to be seen was why and how the Lord would direct him.

The apartment rental he thought was a sure thing had fallen through just yesterday. Tomorrow he'd have to return the truck to the rental agency and put his furniture and most of his belongings in storage. He wouldn't need them. Mabel and Cora offered to give him a room in their home. A smile tugged at his lips. The sisters had been like family to him, at church and at home. It would be like old times.

Ray glanced at the clock on the dash and accelerated. Mabel had told him to pick her up at exactly three thirty in front of the nursing home where she volunteered every Friday. No sense starting off on the wrong foot. When Mabel gave an order, she expected prompt compliance.

Idling at the red light at the corner, he spotted her stocky figure on the sidewalk up ahead, tapped the horn, and waved. Mabel planted her fists on her ample hips. He pulled to the curb, put the truck in PARK, and hopped out.

"Ray Reed, look at the time! You gonna stare all day or help me up into this monstrosity?" Mabel glanced skeptically at the truck, then offered him her arm. "I might need a ladder."

"Hello, Miss Mabel." He kissed her cheek. "No need for a ladder. I'll get you in."

"Hello to you, too." Her dark eyes sparkled, belying her gruff words. "Get a move on. You know what I always say, 'Time is a tool—'"

" 'Not to be wasted,'" he finished and laughed.

"Smarty-pants." She grinned.

Mabel had been ordering him around since the day he stood on tiptoes to see her assisting behind the counter at Cora's sweet shop. Nothing like a command from Mabel to remind him he was home. He'd get his life back on track here. He could feel it in his bones.

Ray helped her into the passenger seat, hopped back into the cab, and merged slowly into traffic. "Thank you for taking me in at the last minute."

She glanced at him. "Kind of impulsive of you to make a last-minute decision to come back, but then you always were kind of impulsive. Besides, I'm glad you're home. Means you're coming back to your senses."

Ray shrugged. "I don't know if that's possible."

She sniffed. "Well, did you get rid of that dangerous motorcycle?"

"Not ready to do that, I'm afraid."

"Where is it?"

"In the back of this truck with my furniture."

"Hmm. Then you're right. You haven't come back to your senses."

He hit a bump in the road, and she grunted.

"Sorry, Miss Mabel. The shocks in these trucks aren't the greatest."

"I can feel that." Mabel massaged her neck. "I'm gonna have to see my chiropractor after this ordeal."

"You still see Dr. . .what's his name? Douglas?"

She nodded. "Sure do. Tom Douglas. And he's still sweet on Cora."

Ray laughed. "They've been sweet on each other as long as

I can remember. I'm surprised they haven't tied the knot."

"Neither of them ever been married. Both scared to death. Silly, is what I think." She snorted. "And not the first ones I know who're scared to fall in love."

Mabel had always been straightforward, but Ray had to ask. "Do you mean me?"

"Oh no. You're not afraid of love; you best fine-tune your con meter, though." She laughed. "Anyway, I'm praising the Lord that you've come back where you belong. You miss home?"

"I'll say." Ray eyed her smooth, mahogany skin. "You look good, Miss Mabel. You never change."

She rolled her eyes. "I'm hoping you changed. You shouldn't of left home to begin with. Just my opinion."

Mabel fanned herself with her ever-present handkerchief, filling the cab of the truck with gardenia perfume. He couldn't help pondering the wisdom of her statement.

"Running away doesn't solve anything." As was her habit, Mabel hummed between sentences. "Yep, trust Old Mabel on that. I did some running in my day 'fore I met my Ralphie."

Mabel's husband had passed away fifteen years ago, yet she often spoke of him as if he were still alive. When encouraged to find another man, she protested that Ralph Peter Sanders had been the love of her life. No one could ever replace him. Ray sighed. What would it be like to have a woman who loved him that much? At one time he thought that woman was Bailey. Perhaps she still could be. Only the Lord knew, but Mabel was right—the time he'd spent in the Tri-Cities had brought him to his senses. The distance made him realize how much he missed his home.

"Speaking of running, you heard from your mama?"

He nodded. "Got an e-mail. She's somewhere in the Middle East covering a story."

"Never could handle her grief over your daddy, always being gone for business." Mabel hummed and nodded. "But you never blamed her none."

"Why would I? I had you and Cora." He glanced at her. "Speaking of careers, I was offered my old job back. I drove up last week to qualify." The thought didn't bring him the joy he thought it should.

Mabel tucked her handkerchief into her pocketbook. "Hm-hm. You were a great cop, and you could do that anywhere." Her dark eyes snapped up to his. "So what really brought you back here? Strange decision after you didn't visit all this time. Even before that, we didn't see much of you. Always dating that. . .what was her name? Sally?"

"Bailey." He was struck with remorse. "I'm sorry I didn't visit. I guess I went through a pretty selfish phase."

She patted him on the knee. "No matter about that," she said briskly. "Happens to everyone. Point is, you're home—and don't avoid the question."

He couldn't fool Mabel. She always managed to figure things out. As a kid he suspected she had a phone line to heaven. Now he knew it was a combination of discernment, experience, and common sense. If he were a hundred percent honest, he'd tell Mabel he wanted his old life back. His life before Bailey Cummings cheated on him with Dwight Connor, a local public defender. But he wasn't up for a sermon.

"I feel like God led me back here." Ray shrugged. "We'll see what happens."

"Uh-huh. I believe the first, but you aren't sayin' everything." She clucked her tongue. "No matter. Truth will tell. And you're in good hands now. Cora fixed up the biggest bedroom for you." Mabel chuckled. "It's gonna be nice having you around, son."

"Thanks for letting me stay. I'm not sure I could have found another rental so last-minute."

She slapped his arm. "If you'd gone anywhere else we would have dragged you back to our place. It's a divine appointment. Besides, you helping Cora and me with the repairs on that old Victorian across the street in trade for room and board is a godsend. We can trust you to do things right."

He smiled. "What made you decide to buy the Victorian? It's going to be a lot of work running a bed-and-breakfast."

She breathed a heavy sigh. "After we sold the candy store we found ourselves with too much time on our hands." Mabel wagged her head. "Idleness is the devil's workshop, you know. So we came up with the idea of a bed-and-breakfast. Ralphie left me very comfortable. Might as well put some of that to good use." She grinned. "I always did have my eye on that place."

"One taste of Cora's cooking and the place will be booked every weekend." Ray lingered at the STOP sign and scanned the canopy of tree branches. "I'll only be staying a few months. Once I get your B&B in shape, I'll rent a place of my own in town."

"Hmm, that old Victorian's gonna take a lot longer than a couple months to fix up."

"Philip and a few friends promised to help."

"Still, a lotta work." She smiled. "But that's good. Cora and I, we're gonna love having your company."

"You sure about that?" Ray laughed. "Remember when Miss Cora beat me over the head with a rolled-up newspaper for stealing—"

"Jelly rings." Mabel's shoulders shook with laugher. "Lord help us all. I thought your daddy was going to do worse than Cora that day. Tan your hide till you couldn't sit." She started laughing again, then rested her hand on his arm. "You were only a kid. A stubborn, willful little boy, but you turned out to be a fine man. Your daddy should see you now."

Ray turned away from her and swallowed past the ache in his throat.

"Here we are," Mabel said as though she needed to point out the cozy Cape Cod where he'd spent more time than he could count as a teen searching for purpose.

"Looks like Cora is home." He pulled up behind their 1960 Thunderbird, went around to the passenger door, and helped her down.

"I'm sorry for bringing up your daddy." Mabel reached up and brushed a finger over his cheek. "The missing never goes away. We just have to trust the Lord to fill the gaps however He sees fit until we see them again."

"You can talk about Dad anytime. It's nice remembering, even though it's sometimes still painful." Arm in arm, Ray walked her to the pristine white picket fence lined with daisies. "He's been gone a long time now."

"Too long. Everybody loved your daddy." She let go of his arm and pointed across the street. "The old Victorian is beautiful, isn't it?"

He nodded. "It will make a great bed-and-breakfast."

"Yes indeedy." Mabel hummed her way up the flagstone path and up the porch steps to the red front door.

Ray began to follow, then stopped and looked around the yard. "Did you hear that?"

"What? I don't hear a thing." Mabel turned and came back down the stairs.

"Some kind of whimpering." Spotting movement in the hedges to his right, he cut across the yard. "What is that?" The low branches stirred, and he hunkered down. Mabel joined him. The whimpering grew louder, and a doe-eyed fur ball limped out. "Look at this," Ray said. "We've got a hurt pup here."

"Oh my," Mabel groaned.

He thought he saw movement out of the side of his eye. He glanced up, but the dog trembled, and he turned his attention back to her. He examined her, but she didn't move to bite him. She stared up into his eyes as though to plead for help. "Poor thing. I'm worried the leg might be broken. We should be careful."

"Looks like one of them little terrier dogs, if you can call something this size a dog. I don't think God made 'em to be this small, like a guinea pig with long legs, but what do I know?" Mabel's eyes and touch were soft, despite her words, and she stroked the dog's tiny head.

Ray picked up the dog and held her in his arms like a baby. "I'd better take her to the animal hospital. Is PetVet still out there on—"

"No, not there! You take that poor baby over to Faith's vet clinic. She'll take care of her."

He started at the name. "Faith? Faith Hart?"

Mabel nodded. "Didn't have time to tell you everything, but while you were exploring your angst, Faith Hart came to town. It's been a long, long time since we seen her. Anyway, she's our neighbor now. She bought her grandmother's old house." She nodded in the direction of a blue-sided two-story next door. "She opened a vet clinic in town while you were gone."

"I figured she was still in the Navy."

"No." Mabel stroked the dog's head. "She didn't do that upping thing they talk about."

"You mean 're-upping' into the military?"

"Yes, that's it."

Ray's mind raced with follow-up questions, but he had to tend to the dog. "Will Faith take me without an appointment?"

"'Course she will." Mabel looked at her wristwatch. "She's open until five tonight, but won't leave until at least six. The door is open anytime she's there, even after hours. Dr. Hart will take good care of the pup." She explained the location of the clinic to him, and Ray headed toward the rental truck.

Doctor Faith Hart. Yes, it made perfect sense. Back in the day during summers with her grandmother, Faith took in every stray in the neighborhood, even box turtles. That's how they'd met—rescuing two sickly kittens from a cardboard box on the side of the road. She had always wanted to be a vet. The warm bundle stirred next to his chest, and he stared into her chocolate eyes, suddenly feeling like a little boy. "Miss Mabel, if Faith can help the dog and we can't find the owner, can we..."

A grin lit her eyes. "As long as you take care of the pup, we'll let you keep her." From the open truck window he thought he heard, "Still the same Ray."

She turned and waved. "Just get home in time for dinner. Cora's got your favorites planned." Mabel was chuckling as he drove off.

two

Faith inspected an acrylic glass enclosure, then looked at Lindsey, the veterinarian assistant. "When's the last time these cages were cleaned?"

The young woman shrugged. "I cleaned them myself not more than two hours ago, Dr. Hart. Birds will be birds."

Faith felt the bite of impatience and took a deep breath. *Lord, help me change. . . .* Her need for cleanliness at the clinic bordered on obsession. It was a burden for her, not to mention her staff, but she couldn't seem to help herself.

"Here." Faith pointed. "Can't you see this? There's bird breath all over the glass."

"Um, bird breath?" Lindsey shrugged again. "You mean those foggy spots?"

Faith released a noisy breath. "Yes, those foggy spots."

The enclosure held a macaw aptly named Nero who squawked like an angry chicken. A very loud chicken. The parrot had been treated with charcoal for munching on a lily from his owner's anniversary bouquet, and he was not a happy bird.

"There's no such thing as bird-breath spots," Lindsey grumbled as she went to the utility cabinet and grabbed a cleaning cloth. "I'll wipe it down *again* and risk my fingers to that carnivore." She glared first at Faith, then at the parrot, who protested his treatment with more vigor.

Faith closed her eyes. *Lord, help me be patient.* She couldn't risk losing Lindsey. The woman was better with animals than people and excelled in the examining room. A little like herself, come to think of it. She prepared to apologize to Lindsey for nit-picking, hoping it would help the woman's mood, when the sound of the bell signaled that someone had entered the clinic.

"Is Gladys still out there?" Hands clasped, Faith resisted the urge to snatch the cloth from Lindsey's hand and clean the cages herself.

"No. She left early to—"

"That's right. I remember now. I'll go see who it is while you finish cleaning." Faith ignored Lindsey's exaggerated sigh, turned, and hurried down the blue-tiled hallway to the reception cubicle. She stopped at the counter, staring at a tall, dark-haired man. He looked vaguely familiar. Handsome. Very. Her gaze dropped to his arms where he cradled a small wire-haired terrier. As straight and tall as she stood from military training and being raised in a military family, she had to look up to meet his gaze.

"How may I help you?"

A broad, warm smile creased his cheeks. She almost laughed at the incongruous sight of the big man holding the small dog.

He chuckled. "Tiny, huh?"

Faith blinked and stared into his eyes. Truth dawned. "Ray?"

"Faith?" They spoke at the same time.

He winked, and her breath caught. For a moment she went dizzy as memories flooded her mind. *Ray!* She dashed around the counter but caught herself before she jerked him into a hug. They stood face-to-face for what seemed an eternity.

"We need to catch up, but I have an emergency here." He held the dog out for her inspection.

Her attention dropped to the tiny creature. "What happened? Is she yours?"

"I don't know what happened to her; and no, she's not," he said. "I found her in the bushes between Mabel and Cora's house and your grandmother's—your house. I'm afraid the leg might be broken."

Faith examined the dog. "I've got a lot of questions for you, but right now you need to follow me. I have to x-ray that leg."

"Look at you," he said as they hurried down the hall to the back where she operated on her patients. "You're a real doctor. A vet."

She snorted. "Yes, well, no big deal."

"No big deal? Of course it's a big deal."

Too bad her father didn't think so. "If you say so, I guess it is. What I do know is it's a lot of work." She pointed where she wanted him to place the dog. "Lindsey!"

"What?" Lindsey snapped from the other room.

Ray's eyebrows rose, but Faith ignored his reaction.

"I need your help sedating this dog."

"I'll help, too, if you need me," Ray offered.

As soon as Lindsey saw the dog, her irritation faded, and she jumped right into her job, directing Ray as well.

"No break," Faith said a few minutes later after examining the x-rays. She was amazed at how comfortable she felt in Ray's presence—how easily they were falling back into a comfortable relationship.

Lindsey bustled around, cleaning up. Faith felt doubly guilty for her earlier impatience. "Lindsey, you go on home now. You'll get overtime for staying late. I'll finish up."

"Okay." The young woman left with one last smile for the small dog.

Ray stroked the dog's tiny, still head. "I'm glad she doesn't have any broken bones."

"Me, too, but I wonder how this happened." She glanced up at Ray. "I'm afraid she's been kicked."

"I hope no one did this deliberately." Ray rubbed the dog's ears between his fingers. "Really sad to think that someone might have hurt this gentle animal."

"Makes me furious." Her stomach clenched. "I see so much animal abuse."

Ray patted her shoulder gently. "I've seen a great deal of all sorts of abuse as a cop. It gets very old. The worst is when it's kids."

Anger tugged at her. She couldn't imagine dealing with child abuse cases. With her temper, she'd be tempted to take on an abuser.

They were silent while she finished her work on the dog.

❧

After washing her hands, Faith turned her attention to Ray. "Cora and Mabel told me you took a break from your job. Is that why? All the bad things you saw? Were you burned out?"

Ray inhaled and shifted uncomfortably. "I guess that was part of it." He shrugged. "It's not as bad as life in New York City, I'm sure, but police work can make one cynical, even in Bothell."

He grew silent, and she decided to try a different conversational direction. "Last I saw you I was sixteen, remember? Dad didn't want me hanging around with a 'rebellious musician.'"

Arms spread, Ray chuckled. "And now I'm a keeper of the law." He looked her up and down, making her want to blush. "You were a couple inches taller than me at the time, but still. . . just as beautiful."

She did blush. "Now you tower over me." She took in his visage again. Standing straight and tall, his thick, dark hair mussed, he was more handsome than ever.

"I missed seeing you during the summers after your dad was transferred from Bremerton to Virginia Beach. Your mom died, then your grandmother moved, too, and I never saw you again." Ray's sincere dark eyes searched hers.

"Mom." Faith sighed. "That kind of change in a teen's life changes everything. But that's why Dad accepted the transfer. And why grandma moved with us. To take care of us in Virginia. She was the saving grace of my life, you know. I missed the freedom of those summers in Bothell." She smiled. "But that's past. Now is now. What were you doing at Mabel and Cora's? Last I heard you'd left town, but my partner just had a baby, and her schedule is erratic. I've been filling in for both of us. I haven't talked to the sisters for over a week."

"I'm going to move in with them."

"Mabel and Cora?" She sounded like a parrot. "Really?"

"It's temporary. The apartment I had lined up didn't work

out at the last minute. We're sort of bartering. I'm going to work on the Victorian they bought in trade for rent."

"Nice. They could use the help." She focused on the terrier.

"I'll pay for everything you did for the dog," Ray said. Always the hero.

"Don't worry about that. I'm not worried about the money as much as I am the dog. I'll put out notices and see if I can find the owner." She tightened her lips. "I will need to determine if they are abusive or if something else happened."

Nodding, Ray moved closer to her. The sight of his guitar-string-calloused fingertips brought on a fresh flood of memories.

Faith returned her gaze to the dog and cleared her throat. "This little girl is an orphan for the moment, so I don't have an owner to call. She seems so fragile. . . ." She considered options. "I really don't want to leave her in the kennel. She'll wake and be terrified. Once she comes out of sedation, I'll take her home with me." She toyed with the idea of inviting Ray over to dinner at her place to catch up.

He glanced at his watch. "I didn't realize the time. I've got to go. Mabel ordered me to be home for dinner. Apparently Cora has something special planned."

Faith covered her disappointment with a laugh. "That sounds like Cora. Leave me your number, and I'll keep you posted about the dog."

Ray rested his hand on her shoulder. "Thanks. So good to see you again, Faith. Or do you want me to call you doctor?"

"Doctor? Between friends?" She smiled up into those dark eyes that seemed to read her.

Ray pulled out his wallet and handed her a business card. "The address is wrong, but that's my cell number."

Smiling, she gave him a mock salute. "You'll be hearing from me."

"Good." His full lips turned up in a slow smile. "Look forward to it."

Faith watched him leave the room. He had been her buddy during the warm summers when she'd stayed in Bothell with her grandmother—until her family moved to Virginia Beach. At the same time he started sending her letters declaring his undying love to her. That scared her, but worse was her father's disapproval. What had she really been thinking at the time? It was hard to remember. She guessed her mother's passing had something to do with that—a sort of grief-induced amnesia. And where had avoiding her father's disapproval gotten her? Since she'd left the military, she was a disappointment to him on every level.

The terrier began to move on the table, and she stroked the pup's bony head and found a piece of glitter on her fingertips. "What did you get into, girl? I think I'm going to name you Sparkles till we find your rightful owner." She smiled. "A perfect name for you since you came from Ray."

Faith hummed as she waited for the dog to fully wake up. She was unaccountably happy. Ray looked good. She closed her eyes and pictured him. No, he looked great. Was he seriously dating anybody? Faith frowned and chastised herself. The clinic took all her time. Her father might see her as the prodigal daughter who didn't re-up in the Navy—but she would show him. She'd make a success of herself. She'd not get sidetracked with romantic notions. But, oh my. Ray Reed—

Faith checked through the messages Gladys had left on her desk. *Your dad called.* He'd also called her cell phone, but she'd ignored it. Her good mood seeped away. The mere thought of her father made her worry she'd done something wrong. As if she were a teenager and had to hide things from him. Like Ray Reed being back in town. How silly was that? Her father had mostly washed his hands of her anyway.

Snap out of it, Faith! She tried to focus on her tiny patient. Ray would be living with Cora and Mabel—a few steps from her house. Faith couldn't restrain a smile.

three

Ray swiped his boots on the outdoor mat, then rang the bell. The red door swung open, and he stepped inside the foyer into Cora's open arms.

"Miss Cora." He kissed her cheek.

"Don't you dare ring the bell," she chided him. "This is your home, you know."

"I've missed you."

"Look at you," she said. "All grown up."

Ray shut the door while he chuckled. "It's not like I've been gone *that* long."

"It's been long enough." She narrowed her dark eyes, so much like Mabel's, and looked him up and down. "You've lost weight."

He stuck his thumbs in his waistband. It was loose. "I had this goofy good friend in the Tri-Cities who fed me health food."

"Bah! Health food." Cora clucked her tongue.

Mabel came bustling up behind her sister and glanced at her watch. "You're right on time. Now, how is that little slip of a dog?"

"Fine. Faith x-rayed that leg. No broken bones." Ray glanced around. Floral paper covered the wall in the hallway, and a gilded mirror hung over a mahogany sideboard. Old fashioned, just like the sisters. There was only one thing new. A gold-framed photo of Mabel and Cora in their Sunday best hanging in a prominent position in the hall.

"Nice." Ray pointed. "Where'd that come from?"

"Faith snapped the picture of us," Mabel said. "Gave it to us last Christmas."

"We're going to put it in the Victorian." Cora tilted her head, studying the photo. "We're calling it Two Sisters' Bed and Breakfast."

"Great name. And I'm impressed with Faith's work."

"It's her hobby," Cora added. "She says it's a good hobby for her. All about perfection."

"She'll sneak up on you and snap a photo faster than you can blink," Mabel warned. "Don't be surprised."

"Hmm." What other things had changed about Faith in the years they'd been out of contact? "Well, the house looks great. Just like I remember." He planted another kiss on each sister's cheek. "And you guys do, too."

"Flattery will get you everywhere." Cora laughed and swatted him with the dish towel she'd had draped over her shoulder.

"You go wash up and come to the table," Mabel ordered. "Supper's ready."

Ray took an appreciative sniff. "Yes, so it is. I'll be right back."

He hurried to the half bath under the stairs, feeling like the prodigal returned. After scrubbing his face and hands in the washroom, he looked in the mirror and found himself smiling. His first day home and things seemed to be working out well. He hoped it was a harbinger of good things to come. Monday he'd be back to work. What was left was to contact Bailey. He'd heard she was no longer seeing Dwight and went to visit her folks in California to recover. Perhaps. . .

He smiled wider. Then there was Faith. What an extra bonus—having his old friend next door.

Ray exited the washroom and went to the butcher-block table in the center of the eat-in kitchen, which was covered with plates of food.

"Is this what you call supper?" He almost forgot what the sisters considered an evening meal. "This is a feast fit for a king. Yum, fried chicken. And sweet potatoes. And mashed potatoes and gravy."

Cora nodded, eyes shining with pride. "Always been your favorites."

Mabel filled his glass to the brim with sweet tea. "Now sit

down, and let's pray before the 'feast' gets cold."

"My pleasure." Ray sat, clasped his hands, and closed his eyes as Mabel uttered solemn words of thanks to God. They said their amens, and the sisters began passing platters. His friend Shannon from the Tri-Cities should see him now. She'd have a cautionary tale about each food group. Shannon with her salads, tofu, and herbal teas.

"So, you saw Faith then?" Mabel's tone was far too casual, which meant she had something to say.

Ray nodded, mouth full, and steeled himself for whatever was coming next.

Cora and Mabel exchanged glances. "She's a good girl," Mabel said. "Tidy, organized, and a good cook."

He didn't need the reminder about her tidiness and organization. Faith's father kept her on a military agenda even as a teen. But the only thing she ever cooked that he remembered was chocolate chip cookies. "I didn't get a chance to ask her how she ended up in Bothell."

"She loved this town. Good memories for her." Mabel waved her fork as she talked.

Cora nodded. "After she opened the clinic, her grand-mother's old house came on the market. She snatched it up in a big hurry. Paid more than it was worth, too."

"When her granny passed, Faith was heartbroken," Mabel said.

Poor Faith. Her grandma's house was the one place she could go to escape and be herself. He could only imagine how her life was after they moved and she no longer had a place to visit. "I remember how much she loved her grandma."

"Yes, that's a fact." Mabel passed him the mashed potatoes. "Eat!"

"Don't be shy." Cora added another crispy chicken leg to his plate. "Last July Faith moved in with us for a couple months while she opened the clinic. Drives us to church, too. Still does. We like to be driven to church on Sunday morning."

"Really?" He stared from one sister to the other. "Don't tell me you let her drive that Thunderbird of yours. You never let me drive it."

Cora studied him with a raised brow. "You're a boy. Reckless."

"I'm a cop. Not reckless."

"High-speed chases," Mabel said.

Ray laughed. "Not if I can help it." He paused. "So Faith goes to Bothell Community Church?"

"Yes, indeed." Cora smiled wide.

"No kidding." Interest piqued, Ray held his tongue while he waited for more.

"Praise God. Faith lost her way for a while, but then she came back to the Lord," Mabel added. "We keep track of kin."

Kin. That's how Mabel and Cora thought of all the kids they'd known and taken in over the years. "I always liked having her around in the summers when we were teenagers." Too late he realized he'd given Cora and Mabel fodder—they were infamous matchmakers.

Cora laughed. "You sure was sweet on her."

Mabel stared at him expectantly.

Yep, this is what he'd signed up for. The sisters would always think of him as a little boy in need of advice. "C'mon, I was a kid. Summer love. Puppy love."

"Puppy love, huh?" Mabel rolled her eyes, then pointed to the front of the house. "You'd be sittin' out there on the porch, strumming your guitar, writing love songs—"

"I was seventeen, Miss Mabel." But they had a point, and Ray couldn't help but laugh. It was the summer of Faith's sixteenth birthday when she said she wouldn't be returning to Bothell for summer vacations. His letters to Faith went unanswered. "I was surprised Faith didn't stay in the Navy."

"Mmm, her daddy was, too. Faith was expected to keep up with her two brothers. Rise in the ranks." Cora sighed. "Make the old man proud."

"Poor girl." Mabel dropped a second helping of buttered beans onto his plate. "Four years in the Navy. Honorable discharge. Went to vet school. Opened a clinic." She sniffed.

"Not good enough for her papa."

"I'd tell him a thing or two," Cora murmured.

"Can't tell you the times I've wanted to call him," Mabel said. "He should be ashamed."

Sympathy stirred in his heart for his friend. "It hurts when you can't be yourself." Ray set down his fork. "Remember when I used to say I wanted to be a musician? I must've sounded like a fool."

"Musician would have suited you, too," Mabel said. "You just didn't have anywhere to do it."

"Some people take to their jobs like a duck to water." Cora chuckled. "Your brother. . .oh, that Philip was gung ho about law enforcement." Both sisters laughed.

"He still is—probably more than me." Ray thought about Faith again and smiled. "I'm glad it all worked out for Faith. She got her wish to become a vet."

"She's beautiful." Cora leveled a gaze at him. "And you two might want to pick up where you left off." She wiggled her eyebrows. "I'm just saying."

"No, no." He had to make his position clear. Nip the matchmaking in the bud. "I'm hoping I can patch things up with—"

"No!" Cora said.

"Oh my, you don't mean. . .*her*." Mabel's fork hit her plate with a loud clank. "That Sally up and left you for another man. How could you ever trust her again?"

"Her name's *Bailey*." The reminder was like a knife to his heart. Ray released a pent-up breath. "It was partly my fault. I was too focused on my job. I didn't give Bailey the time she needed. I should've—"

Mabel's incredulous glare and Cora's open mouth rendered him silent.

"Such a thing as *faithfulness*," Mabel muttered.

"And being too trusting." Cora nodded.

The doorbell rang, and Ray rocketed out of his chair. "I'll get it," he said, relieved to dodge the subject of Bailey and her infidelity. Had he been too trusting in his personal life? Hadn't being a cop taught him anything?

Ray opened the door. Faith stood there. She had shed her medical jacket, and the deep blue of her blouse emphasized the depth of her brown eyes.

"Hello?" A tiny worried frown wrinkled her brow. "May I—"

"Sure. Come on in." Ray stepped aside. Faith had been a pretty teen, but now. . .

"Who is it?" Mabel called from the kitchen.

"Faith!" He cleared his throat.

"Faith, honey, you come on in here," Cora yelled. "We haven't seen you in too long."

"Guess I'd better." Faith shut the door behind her. "I have a question, and I need to ask them as well as you."

"How's the puppy?" he asked on their way down the hall.

"I've got her tucked in at my house. She'll be fine." At the door to the kitchen, she grinned up at him and her eyes narrowed with humor. "I named her Sparkles for old time's sake."

"Like the stuffed alien bear with sparkly antennas that I won at the fair for you when you were fourteen? You remember that?"

She nodded. "Not only do I remember that, but I still have her. And other things."

"Really?" He kept a plastic bin full of things Faith had given him over the years, too. It warmed his heart to know he still meant something to her.

four

Faith straightened her blouse as she walked in the kitchen and made sure it was tucked into her jeans. She greeted the sisters with a smile. "I'm sorry to interrupt your dinner. I didn't even change before I came over."

"Don't you dare get formal with us," Mabel said. "Sis, why don't we set another place at the table?"

"Miss Cora, don't do that. I appreciate the offer, but I can't stay." Faith avoided Ray's gaze. For reasons she couldn't fathom she felt like a jittery schoolgirl around her old friend. "I actually came by to ask if you guys stopped over today or anybody saw suspicious activity around my house."

Ray stepped into her line of vision. "Why? What's wrong?"

Faith searched his concerned eyes. Just like old times. Nobody messed with her during her summertime visits to Bothell. Not with Ray Reed around. She waved her hand in a nonchalant gesture. "No big deal really, but I believe somebody was in my screened-in porch, maybe my house."

"What? And you didn't call the police?" Ray frowned at her.

"'Course she did." Mabel eyeballed him. "She's here, ain't she?"

"Well, I'm not in uniform," Ray said.

"Don't matter," Mabel shot back.

"Hmm-hmm, you'd better have a look, Ray." Cora glanced at Mabel.

"I'd say so." Mabel nodded her agreement. "You go on over there now, son."

Faith studied the two with narrowed eyes. They weren't. . . matchmaking, were they? They had a reputation for that kind of thing.

"Never know these days," Mabel quickly added. "No sense taking any chances."

Faith's shoulders relaxed. Of course they weren't match-making. They knew her situation, and during their last heart-to-heart conversation, they'd concurred there was nothing wrong with staying single to focus on career goals.

"I'll go check it out." Ray took his plate to the sink. "Ladies, thank you so much for the delicious meal. I'll help you clean up as soon as I get back."

"You bet you will or I'll have your hide," Cora said, and she and Mabel laughed.

Ray held open the front door. "They're laughing, but I think Cora's serious."

Faith snickered. Ray was adorable with the feigned worried look on his face. "Cora could still take you. Mabel, too."

"No doubt." He walked behind her through a break in the hedge between her house and the sisters'. The same little opening they had used when they were teens.

"Nice truck." He nodded at her blue Chevy. "Is that your clinic name on the side?"

"Yep. Hart and Downey Veterinarian Clinic." She laughed. "Our last names. Original, huh?"

"The truck is good advertising."

"Exactly."

They reached the gate that led to her backyard, which was surrounded by a split rail fence that was covered on the inside with chicken wire.

"This wasn't here when your grandmother owned the place."

"No. I had it put up after I moved in. Sometimes I'll bring home a dog from the clinic, like I did with Sparkles. Or one of my friends in rescue work will need a temporary place for a dog. It's easier with a fence."

He pointed at an open padlock hanging on the gate. "Do you usually keep this locked?"

"Most of the time." She glanced at the padlock. "I guess I forgot last time I was out here. And someone who is determined could climb the fence. It's not that tall. I just keep it locked so kids can't get back here when I'm keeping dogs."

They stepped through the gate into her backyard. "Where's the puppy?"

Faith's cheeks heated. "In my bedroom in a crate. I know. I'm a sucker."

"Like those kittens you nursed back to health." Ray laughed. "Remember? You let them sleep with you in bed at your grandmother's every night for a week until your father visited and discovered them."

"Yeah. I still can't stand to see an animal hurting, but I don't sleep with them anymore—at least ones I don't know." She bit her lip. "Remember Dad said I'd get fleas or mange? Turns out he was partially right, but I didn't care."

He smiled. "Reminds me of old times. You going on and on about taking care of animals."

"Was I obnoxious?"

"No, it's one of the things I loved about you." Ray gave her a nudge. "I knew we were simpatico ten minutes after we met."

She felt warmed by the reminder. They had been that. Attached from the very beginning. She pointed at the porch door. "Well, this is the scene of the crime."

He glanced around the porch. "Okay, I know this might sound offensive, but did you lock this outside door?"

Faith bit her nail and shrugged. "I guess I wasn't so concerned about this since the gate is usually locked."

His single raised eyebrow said it all.

"I know it's stupid," she said. "And it's weird. I'm so picky about most things, but locks on doors? It's like a brain burp or something."

"Brain burp." He laughed. "Well, everyone has quirks. Yours might as well be burping."

His understanding smile sent warmth through her.

She watched as Ray examined the door to the enclosed porch. His glance slid toward her. "Truthfully, this lock wouldn't be that hard to get through for anyone determined."

"Most houses wouldn't be hard to get into for anyone

determined, locked or not," she countered.

"True enough," he agreed.

She swiped an imaginary speck of dust from the glass top of the wicker table and glanced around, fighting a tiny bit of anxiety.

He noticed. "Why do you think someone was here?"

"See that can of birdseed?" Faith pointed at a large tin next to the back door. "I go out every day and put seed in the bird feeder in the backyard. The can was moved."

He pointed at a round indentation where the can originally sat. "You're sure you didn't accidentally kick it or something?"

She shrugged. "I'm not, no. That's why I didn't call the police. I feel stupid."

"Don't," he said. "You know your habits, and I trust your instincts."

She smiled and watched him look around, heart light that he still had faith in her.

"Was anything missing?"

"If there was, it was nothing important. That's the odd part." Faith shook her head and sighed. "I might be missing a banana and an apple, but then I start to question myself. Did I eat them? I might forget locks, but it seems I would know if someone had taken something."

"Right." Ray scanned the porch and nodded. "I can see that. There's a place for everything. Spotless."

Faith's face warmed as she followed his gaze. Did he see her as a neurotic nitpicker, same as the clinic staff?

"Take me inside and show me around the kitchen."

She opened the back door.

"This was unlocked, too?"

"Yes, I think so," she said. "And all the locks are original to the house. No one changed them."

They stepped into her kitchen. The green walls immediately soothed her.

"Nice," he murmured as he looked around the kitchen.

"There's the bowl of fruit." She nodded at the table. "I'm

pretty sure something is missing."

Ray studied the room, then sighed.

She pulled back a chair from the table. "Would you like to sit?"

Ray took a seat, and Faith settled in a chair directly facing him.

"If my father didn't teach me 'a place for everything, and everything in its place,' four years in the Navy reinforced it."

"Well, it's not a bad thing." Ray's tone was comforting, and she smiled. "Case in point, my friend Shannon back in the Tri-Cities came close to losing her business, a junk shop sort of, and all because. . ." Ray looked thoughtful, like he was searching for a nice way of making his point. "Shannon had a hard time with 'a place for everything, and everything in its place.'"

Faith couldn't hold back a laugh. "Sounds like a real character."

"You guys would get along great," he said.

"Is she your. . .um." She paused. "Sorry. That's not my business."

"No, she's not my girlfriend." He laughed long and hard. "She'd be so amused to hear that. She's a wonderful friend, and she's engaged to a nice guy."

"Good. I mean, good for her." She looked into his eyes, then quickly glanced away, realizing what a good friend she'd lost when she never returned his letters. "Anyway, this break-in stuff may be the work of teen pranksters."

"Yes, or it might be more serious. I'm officially back to work at the Bothell Police Department Monday. Then I can make a suspicious activity report, but that's all I can do right now. I can't file an official report based on the incidents that have occurred so far but if it happens again, we'll have note of it." He leaned toward her. "You need to remember to lock your doors."

"I will." Her cheeks burned, and she looked down at the floor.

"Sorry. Don't mean to make you feel bad."

She rubbed the toe of her sneaker on the floor. "Thank you."

"It's good to see you again," he said softly, then he inhaled.

"I've always wanted to know. Why didn't you write back to me?"

Her gaze snapped up to meet his.

"After you moved to Virginia Beach. You never wrote me like you promised before you left town."

She frowned. How to explain this without telling him the truth? That his intense letters declaring his love scared her to death at a point in her life when nothing made sense. And to make things even harder was the scowl on her father's face when he handed her Ray's letters.

"My father, I guess." Faith looked down at her hands, folded in her lap, remembering the comments her father had made about the "shiftless musician."

"Let me guess." Ray stretched out his long legs and strummed his fingers on the chair arms. "Your dad told you to stay away from me, right?"

She met Ray's dark gaze. "He was trying to control me. He always has."

"Hey, no big deal. It was natural for a career Navy man not to want a longish-haired musician for his daughter." Ray laughed good-naturedly.

Tears stung the backs of her eyes. Father dearest. He had always been overbearing.

"Well, that was his prerogative as your father." Ray shrugged. "It happened a long time ago. He was trying to protect you. And you have to admit, I was pretty intense at that point. It would frighten any father."

And me, too.

"It was infatuation on my part, and it's okay." He smiled at her. "And now you're doing what you always dreamed of." Ray leaned forward and placed his finger under her chin, forcing her to look at him. "Faith Hart. A vet. A real doctor."

A breeze from the overhead fan ruffled his thick, dark hair and raised goose bumps on her arms. She forced her father from her mind and concentrated on her friend. "How about you? Did you buck the system along the way?"

"Afraid not. I was an angel." Ray held his thumbs and

index fingers above his head to make a pretend halo. "Graduated from guitar to harp—for a while."

Faith giggled. She felt fifteen again.

"Seriously, I went into police work like my granddad, father, and brother. The closest I came to bucking the system was the sabbatical I took last year. I spent time in the Tri-Cities. That's when I met Shannon."

"What did you do to support yourself there?"

A grin flashed across his lips. "Besides using my savings, I gave guitar lessons and played for a Christian coffeehouse. Let's just say I lived cheap and lost weight." He winked at her. "But I didn't grow my hair long to save at the barber."

"Well, there's a good thing. You didn't totally go off the deep end." She paused and studied her old friend. "So, you're still a musician?"

He nodded, and she thought she detected confusion in his eyes, but it disappeared.

"A musician, yes, but I need to make money, so. . .I'm back." He spread his arms wide. "I'm ready to continue the family legacy of police work. For the time being."

She laughed. "Your family must be proud of you, Ray."

"My mother, when I hear from her, is supportive. Philip is ecstatic that I'm back."

"I'm looking forward to seeing Philip again. I remember him being so tall and more than a bit intimidating."

"Well, he's still tall."

Faith giggled again.

"And he can still be intimidating, especially to the bad guys." Ray looked at her long and hard. "So how about you? I'm sure your family is proud of you. It's no small feat becoming a vet."

Faith stood abruptly. "I think my brothers are proud of me. My father. . ." She didn't intend the sarcasm in her voice.

The chair scraped the tile floor, and Ray was beside her, open hand on her shoulder. "Sounds like things are still strained between you guys."

She pulled away from him. "My father hasn't changed, if that's what you mean." Her words sounded harsh.

Ray shifted and bit his lip.

"I'm sorry." Faith waved her hand and attempted a smile. "I have to let bygones be bygones."

"Nah, no explanation necessary. I'm working on that myself. A long story." He glanced at his watch. "Um, listen, I've got to get back, unpack some of my stuff. Just let me know what I can do to help with the dog. Like pay you?"

She considered that. "I'm not sure. Let's see if we can find her owner first. If not, we'll make some sort of deal. You were just a Good Samaritan. I hate to make you pay."

"And I hate to make you work for free."

She grinned at him. "Impasse."

He returned her smile. "Back at you."

How easy it was to fall back into familiarity.

"So, let's make time to talk, okay?"

Faith nodded. She was tempted to ask him to stay, if only for a few more minutes, but she had no reason. "I'm glad we're neighbors."

Ray winked. "Me, too." He glanced around the porch as he backed toward the door. "I'll do what I can about the possible break-in."

Faith gave him a thumbs-up. "Sounds good. See you tomorrow."

She watched as Ray crossed the lawn until he was out of sight. "I *am* glad we're neighbors," she whispered.

five

The phone woke Faith at 6:00 a.m. Saturday morning. Only two people called her that early—her father or her partner, Debbie. Faith guessed this time it was the former since she'd forgotten to return his call. Would that be called a Freudian slip?

Reluctantly she picked up the phone. Before she got out a hello, her father reprimanded her. "Why didn't you call me back?"

"I'm sorry, Dad, but I'm busy with—"

"Your clinic."

His harsh tone made her shoulders go ramrod straight.

"No matter. I've got good news. Great news. Your brother, Richard, just made Master Chief. See what happens when you stick to it?"

Faith sighed. Richard had mentioned that he was studying for that, but she'd forgotten. They hadn't communicated in more than a month, and even when they did, it was just surface stuff. So what was the proper response to her father? An apology for disappointing him? Again? "That's great, Dad. I'll e-mail him on board ship to congratulate him."

"You can do it in person, too. The carrier will be back in Bremerton in another month."

Faith continued to look out the bedroom window, watching a red-haired child skirt the trees along the street. She thought it was a girl, but couldn't be sure. The kid disappeared behind a hedge, peeked out, and seemed to look directly at her. Strange. It was pretty early for a youngster to be out and running around, but there were a lot of families with children on the street. And she remembered times during summer vacation when she and Ray would sneak out before breakfast, sit under

33

the trees, and play in the dirt.

Her mind turned, trying to figure out what her father wanted. "Maybe I can drive over there and take everyone out to dinner." The child was still looking at her before she took off down the street, glanced over her shoulder at her house again, then disappeared.

"Your sister-in-law is already planning something," Dad said. "If you're not too busy with that clinic of yours, I'm sure Richard would appreciate you coming. You don't live so far away that you couldn't drive there."

When Faith hung up the phone, her shoulders sagged. She always felt drained after a conversation with her father. Hard as she tried to adhere to "Honor thy parents," a battle raged within to keep negative thoughts of him at bay. He'd gotten so much worse after her mother passed away—pushy, demanding, controlling. So much so that she was glad he lived in Oregon, hours away. She didn't have to see him regularly. And her clinic offered a great excuse to keep her distance. How awful to feel this way about her flesh and blood. She felt like an utter failure. Even Ray, the soulful musician, had continued the family legacy of police work.

Faith grabbed her laptop from her briefcase, turned it on, and opened her e-mail program. There she noticed an e-mail from her brother telling her about his promotion. She jotted a quick congratulations back to him. Then she went to the bedroom window that faced the side yard between her house and the sisters' place. Gazing across the yard, she forced her mind to good things. Like the fact that Ray was back in town. She sighed. This was the perfect time for a walk. That always improved her mood. She turned back to her bedroom and wondered if Ray was still in the habit of waking early and walking. Back when she came to visit her grandma in the summer, he joined her almost every morning. But Grandma claimed Ray only went for morning strolls when Faith was in town. Grandma had that glint in her eye that spoke much more. A little like the glint in Mabel's and Cora's eyes.

But that was then and this was now, and she and Ray had moved on. Faith changed into her walking shorts and a T-shirt, then made her bed, squaring the corners. Afterward she tidied the room and headed downstairs and outside.

While leaning over the porch rail to do her warm-up exercises, she heard a voice and jumped.

"Sorry I scared you." Ray backed away, hands raised. "I was eating breakfast and wondered if you still walked in the mornings, so I came outside to check."

Her heart warmed, realizing he still remembered. *He's really my friend,* Faith thought. "Yep, and I still fast walk."

"Mind if I join you?"

Faith tilted her head. "Sure. I'm headed to the Burke-Gilman Trail. You ready?"

❧

Keeping pace with the trim and in-shape Faith was heart-pounding exercise, something Ray enjoyed. "I've gotta watch what I eat, or I won't be able to do this anymore. I overdid it again last night. Cora and Mabel—"

"You can't live with them and not gain weight unless you make the effort." Faith laughed. "The couple of months I lived there I gained fifteen pounds and couldn't snap my jeans."

Ray laughed. "You'd never know it looking at you now." She was as near perfect as any woman he'd ever laid eyes on.

"Thanks for that." Faith's shy smile reminded him of all he'd missed about her friendship in the years gone by. He pointed to a grassy area and asked, "Wanna sit for a while?"

"Wimp." She poked him in the stomach and laughed. "Race you to that tree."

They reached the large Western hemlock at the same time. Faith laughed and dropped to the grass. He joined her.

"I love this trail and its history. Cool how it used to be part of a railroad." She glanced around, then leaned back against the tree trunk. "Funny how time changes things, but sometimes if we build on the pleasant part of the old, something good comes of it."

"Pretty philosophical for a Saturday morning." Ray tilted back his head and let the July sun warm his face. "This feels good, Faith." Being with her reminded him of summertimes when they were kids. As though he were escaping—a vacation almost.

"Yeah, it's a gorgeous day."

"Right, but I meant being with you feels good. Like old times, huh?" He looked over at her and caught the hint of a blush on her oval face. Maybe it was the hard walking, but he had to know. "Do I make you feel uncomfortable?"

"What? No!" Faith shook her head, and her long, dark ponytail bounced with the action. "Why'd you ask?"

Ray shrugged. "We've been friends forever. You'd tell me if I changed—grew up to be too serious. Right?"

A small frown furrowed her brow. "You? Too serious? You were the most laid-back, mellow guy I knew." Faith tilted her head. "You're asking for a reason, though. What? Somebody accuse you of being a stuffed shirt?"

He should've known she'd get right to it. Ray shrugged. "Not exactly, but I was seeing someone. . .actually engaged to her, and—"

"Oh." An odd look crossed Faith's features. "Don't know why, but that took me by surprise. Go on, please."

He hesitated. "Nah. It can wait." It was too soon to spill the story about Bailey and him. "I'd rather we talk about you." Ray smiled to lighten the mood. "Why didn't you re-up in the Navy? What brought you to that decision?"

"Um, okay, change of topic. Mental whiplash." Faith squinted and rubbed the back of her neck.

He chuckled. "Well, it is a serious question."

"And you ask me as if you've got a serious reason for wanting to know."

Ray shrugged. "I might, I'm not sure."

"Okay, you know I've always loved animals."

"Always. Can't think of a day you didn't have one creature or another occupying your grandma's house."

"Promise you won't laugh." Faith's gentle brown eyes searched his as though for sincerity.

"You know me better than that," Ray said.

"Short story—I had a defining God moment."

Ray crossed his arms over his chest. "I want to hear the long story. I've got time."

Faith looked pensive for a moment, then nodded. "I was on board ship and had to decide whether to re-up or not. My father was pushing me, of course, but to be honest, I didn't mind being in the Navy. He had retired and moved to Oregon, and he seemed to want to continue his career through his kids. The problem was, I didn't feel totally fulfilled. Something was missing, so I began to attend church services and seek the Lord." A tiny grin played on her lips. "I remember those years of Mabel and Cora talking about God's leading." She turned and fully faced him. "Anyhow, we were in port in Spain, and I was walking along, just praying to myself as my friends joked around." She looked off into the distance, as though reliving the moment. "The sun was going down, and I saw this beautiful white stucco church. I stood riveted as the sun hit it at such an angle that a stained-glass tree filled with birds was all I could see." Faith's gaze returned to him. "And I knew, Ray, it was a message from God. He takes care of every sparrow. Maybe it sounds weird, but if God loves the animals enough to take care of them, it's okay if I do, too. Not only that, but then He would take care of me as well."

He sat looking at her for a long moment. "That's beautiful, Faith. I pray He gives me a vision like that for my life."

Faith reached out and almost touched his face but pulled her hand back. "Me, too." She got up and summoned him with a wave of her hand. "Enough rest time. We've got some ground to cover."

Ray nodded, but couldn't take his eyes off his amazing friend. One day she'd make some guy very, very happy.

six

Ray paced the kitchen, cell phone to his ear. "All right, I'll talk to you this afternoon. Enjoy your morning with your folks." He ended the call and put the phone on his belt, then he pulled it back and shut it off. He didn't want the phone ringing in the middle of the church service.

"I know that wasn't Faith," Mabel said behind him.

He turned. "Sneaking up on me? Spying on me?" For a woman of her size, Mabel was as quiet as a cat.

"Ray Reed, you know better." She dropped her pocketbook and Bible on the table and faced him in silence.

He sighed. She was waiting for an answer to her unspoken question. "No, it wasn't Faith. It was Bailey."

"Oh well, then you don't know that Faith can't come to church today. Now you can drive us."

"He'll do it?" Cora asked as she walked into the kitchen.

"Of course I'll drive you to church, ladies. I'll have to drive your car, though. No room on my bike."

"I should say so." Mabel checked her earrings.

Ray stood at the kitchen counter, gulped the last of his coffee, then put the empty cup in the sink. "So Faith drives you every Sunday morning, eh?"

Cora nodded and put a lace hankie in her black purse. "When we're so gussied up, we like to have someone else do the driving."

"Like a chauffeur?" Ray asked.

"Like the man of the house, so don't be a smarty-pants." Mabel reached over and straightened his tie even though it wasn't crooked.

Ray summoned a casual tone. "Faith had to go into the clinic today, huh?"

"Yes." Mabel took a lint roller from a drawer in the kitchen and ran it over her skirt. Then she began to run it over Ray's suit jacket. "Lift your arms."

He obeyed as he stifled a laugh, but his thoughts quickly veered toward Faith's safety. "You know, I think I'm going to let Faith keep that doggy. If anybody tries to break in while she's home—God forbid—at least the dog will bark. She can dial 911 right away."

Cora eyed him. "She wouldn't need no dog to protect her if she had a husband."

Ray scowled. "And I suppose it's my fault that she doesn't have a husband."

"There you go being a wise guy again," Mabel said as she finished with his suit. "Well, don't you worry, you'll see Faith later. We told her to join us for lunch today if she could."

Ray turned and looked at the smiling saint. "I wasn't worried, Miss Mabel. I'm only surprised she went into work today because you told me her clinic was open Monday to Saturday."

"Yes, but her partner's baby is sick, there was an emergency, and their fill-in vet couldn't make it either." Mabel examined her image in the small mirror hanging on the wall and adjusted her frilly lavender hat. Cora came up beside her and said, "Don't be a mirror hog, sister."

"That's the pot calling the kettle black," Mabel retorted.

Ray held back a laugh. Did other women at Bothell Community still wear such amazing creations on their heads? "Ready yet, ladies?"

Two sets of dark eyes snapped to his face as though he'd interrupted a solemn ritual. "I'm not rushing you," Ray quickly added.

Cora grabbed her keys off the kitchen table and dangled them in front of Ray. "Go warm up the car. You look like you've got ants in your pants."

Mabel glanced at her watch. "We've still got plenty of time."

That was priceless, coming from Mabel. But he did feel

antsy even though it was early. Ray went out to the garage and pulled open the door. Perhaps he could talk the sisters into getting an automatic garage door opener. He stood there admiring the shiny old black Thunderbird. It still looked like new. They had a mechanic who appreciated classics and kept the car in mint condition. He turned the key in the ignition, and the engine roared to life. V-8 and powerful. He had a sudden boyish desire to take it out and see just how fast it could go. Not exactly the best thought for a grown man, let alone a cop.

While the car idled, Ray got out and leaned against the door, arms crossed over his chest. He couldn't help but look in the direction of Faith's house. Too bad she wasn't able to attend church with them. Truth be told, he'd been looking forward to visiting church with her, catching up again on old times. Just as friends. Not that Cora or Mabel would buy that story.

The two sisters walked from the house, arms filled with their pocketbooks and large Bibles.

"What were you looking at?" Cora asked when she reached him.

Ray's gaze shot in her direction. "I'm. . .nothing. I was warming up the car."

"And checkin' out Faith's house." Mabel stood beside the back door of the car next to her sister. "We're ready."

Ray opened the door for them. "What? You're both riding in the back? Like I really *am* your chauffeur?"

No response. Cora slid in beside Mabel. "Go on, now, we know you want to drive this baby."

"Since you were knee-high to a grasshopper," Mabel added.

"Yes, ma'ams." He got in and adjusted the seat and rearview mirror to his height. "You never let me drive this 'baby' before. Why now?"

"We're gonna trust you not to drive it like you did that hot rod Mustang you used to own." Cora grunted, then laughed. "Remember that thing?"

"How many tickets did you get?" Mabel asked. "Five?"

"Um, one." Ray paused. "Well, two if you count the parking violation."

Cora clucked her tongue. "Scalawag."

Ray laughed. The fifteen-minute drive to Bothell Community Church went by in a flash as they continued to reminisce. Ray pulled into a spot at the church, helped the sisters out of the car, and looked intently at the A-frame building where he came to know Jesus at age fifteen. Lord knew he was headed for trouble before that day, but his life had taken an amazing turn for the best.

Cora and Mabel walked in, and Ray followed. Most of the congregation was seated already, but he received a warm welcome in the form of smiles and waves.

He sat in a pew three rows from the front, Cora on one side and Mabel on his other. Soon they were joined by Tom Douglas, who sat on Cora's far side. Ray exchanged a smiling glance with Mabel, who just smiled back knowingly and hummed a soft tune.

While they waited for church to start, he glanced around the building. It had changed little. The stained-glass windows still threw color on the walls as the morning sun flowed through them. His gaze paused at one—Jesus carrying a sheep. Memory hit him like a hammer. That was the window he'd stared at during his dad's funeral. Ray had wished he could be a lamb and get carried away from the funeral service. To a green place where his father was still alive. Where everyone could be happy. The sky was filled with dark angry clouds during the graveside service, like Ray's heart. His mother's face was white and devoid of any emotion, as if she had become an empty shell when her husband died. Ray had watched his brother Philip's face for any sign that it was all right to cry. But Philip, then eighteen, stood strong and stoic, and so Ray, ten years old, clenched his jaw and swallowed a gallon of tears. That's when his Sunday school teacher, Mabel, had appeared from nowhere and hugged him from behind while Cora wrapped her arm around his mother's shoulders.

Mabel patted his arm, bringing him back to the present. "You okay, son?"

"Yeah." What had brought on all this remembering? Seeing Faith again? No matter. All was good. He put his hand over hers and with his other grabbed Cora's. "Thank you," he said softly. "I love you guys." And as if they knew what he meant, they squeezed his hands in return.

Pastor Gary Underwood stood at the altar, and Ray focused his full attention on the minister who knew how to rightly divide the Word of God. He loved most when Pastor Gary would take a word or two from Hebrew or Greek and get to the deepest core of a verse's original meaning.

"I'll get to the sermon in a sec," the pastor said, "but first I've got a request." He looked out over the congregation, smiling. "Why do you all look worried? No, I'm not going to ask for volunteers or take an extra offering." After the laughter subsided, the pastor continued. "Bothell Community is in dire need of a full-time music minister. As most of you know, we haven't been able to fill that slot since our brother, Kenny, retired due to illness." Pastor Gary paused and took a breath. "We need someone who knows music. Someone who can get along with people and flow with the church membership and leadership. Someone with a heart to worship God."

Ray inhaled.

"So please, pray on it, saints. We'll pray in unison now, and if the Lord stirs up the desire in your heart, please get back to me."

From the side of his eye, Ray saw Mabel glance at him, but he stared straight ahead. He was afraid if he looked at her, he'd be unable to contain his desire to run to the front of the church and accept the position on the spot.

seven

After the service, Tom took Cora's arm and walked her to the back door.

Mabel watched them. "Some folks just don't know when the time is right to step into what God has for them."

Ray glanced at her, but she had already started down the aisle. Had she been referring to Tom and Cora?

At the back door, the pastor and his wife, Nicole, greeted Mabel warmly. Then Pastor Gary turned to Ray and smiled. "Welcome back, son. You still play that guitar?"

"Yes, I do."

"If I called you to fill in, would you mind?"

Ray's heart beat faster. "Not at all."

Pastor Gary smiled, gave Mabel a hug, and moved to the next person.

Ray headed home with the sisters in near silence until Mabel slapped his shoulder from the backseat. "What's wrong, son?"

"Probably my imagination running away with me."

"What're you imagining?" Cora asked.

"I thought I was supposed to go back to law enforcement." Ray nodded to reassure himself. "I mean, look at how things worked out. But something strange happened in the service. . . while we prayed about the ministry position." He blew out a long breath and tried to shake off the feeling. "I'm a cop. I couldn't work full-time as a music minister."

"Hmm." Cora began to hum.

"The Lord give you a nudge?" Mabel asked.

"A nudge? It was more like a shove, which makes me wonder." Ray wagged his head. "No. . .I don't. . .no." He took a deep breath. "I think that punch of desire I felt in the service was my own wishful thinking. I have to be responsible. I have a job to do. I'm not a kid anymore with dreams of being a rock star."

"A rock star?" Mabel repeated, and both sisters broke into laughter.

He glanced into the rearview mirror. "What'd I say that's so funny?"

Cora slapped his shoulder this time. "A music minister is a far cry from a rock star. C'mon now!"

"But he's that good, don't you think?" Mabel asked.

"Yes indeedy," Cora said.

"Thank you," Ray said in his best Elvis voice. "Thank you very much."

Mabel came as near to giggling as he'd ever heard her. They were still laughing when Ray pulled into the driveway, then cut the engine.

"We're going to fix lunch." Cora exited the car and started up the walk.

Mabel took off her hat. "Ray, you go on and sit on the porch. You got some thinking to do. We'll call you when it's ready."

"Ask Him what He wants you to do." Cora pointed skyward before she entered the house.

Ray changed into jeans and a T-shirt, then sat on the porch swing and let the soles of his sandaled feet scuff on the wood porch floor. Had the Lord given him the stirring in his heart when the pastor mentioned a music minister? Or was it Ray's own desire? If the Lord was the One who'd given him the desire, leading him to apply for the position, he couldn't refuse. He'd been out of His will on other occasions and lived to regret it.

"Lord, please make Your desire clear. In the meantime, I'm going to keep heading in the direction I began."

He pushed the swing and noticed a kid wearing a baseball cap standing on the sidewalk in front of Faith's house. He squinted. Looked like a little girl. Probably from the neighborhood, but why was she staring at Faith's place? He immediately thought of someone being in Faith's house, and he stood. The girl noticed him and took off running down the street.

Ray jumped off the swing and started down the stairs, but the girl was out of sight before he could follow. The phone rang inside, and he heard the hum of Mabel's voice as she answered it. He strolled the front yard, then walked to the back, checking things out. Between the sisters' house and Faith's, he noticed some of the chicken wire was coming loose from the fence. He heard the sound of a truck engine. Faith was home. Maybe he'd offer to help her staple it back on. He walked around front and waited as Faith exited her truck, waved, and walked toward him.

"What are you doing in my yard?" she asked, smiling. "Trespassing?"

He saluted her. "I'm from the police. I'm investigating."

Her brows rose. "Investigating?"

"Ma'am, did you know you have loose chicken wire on your fence?"

"Oh dear." She pressed her fingers to her lips in mock horror. "Is that a crime?"

He glanced at the sky, pretending to think. "Well, no, not if you get someone to help you fix it soon."

Faith clasped her hands. "Oh, officer, are you offering to help?"

"Well, it's above and beyond the call of duty, but. . ."

"I'd be ever so grateful." She glanced at him and batted her eyelashes.

He laughed, and she joined him. Soon they were out of breath.

When he'd finally caught his breath, he smiled at her. "I'd be glad to help you mend the fence. Just let me know when."

"Okay."

He frowned. "Now on to something more serious. I saw this kid hanging around your house."

Faith grimaced. "You're thinking of the break-in, aren't you?"

"Sort of. Well, yeah."

"We have lots of kids in the neighborhood."

"This one had on a ball cap. I think it was a girl—"

"Shorter hair?" she asked. After Ray nodded, Faith said, "I've seen her, too. Would a kid do this?"

"Kids are capable of a lot more than you think. They can be as bad as adults."

"Lunch is ready," Mabel called from the back porch.

"I'm going to run in and check on Sparkles. Tell the sisters I'll be right there."

☙

Faith strolled into Mabel and Cora's kitchen, sniffing the air appreciatively. "Ham?"

"Yes," Cora said, waving a wooden spoon in the air. "Both of you wash your hands."

Ray grinned at Faith. "Race you to the bathroom."

He got there first and wouldn't let her near the sink.

"No fair," she said. "You had a head start."

"Gotta take the advantages given to us." He flicked water at her.

She reached under his arm, put her hand under the running water, and flicked him back. Soon their faces were dripping.

"Children!" Mabel called. "Stop that fooling around and come to the table."

Ray and Faith were still grinning, faces damp, when they got to the kitchen.

"My lands, you'd think these two were teenagers again." Cora placed a heaping bowl of rolls on the table.

"Mmm-hmm." Mabel smiled.

Faith was about to drop into her regular chair when Cora tapped her arm and pointed to an empty seat next to Ray. Still matchmaking. She exchanged a quick grin with Ray. He saw it, too. Oh well. No harm could come from their efforts.

"Let's pray," Mabel said when everyone was seated.

While they ate, they discussed Faith's break-ins.

"You think it might be a child?" Mabel asked, eyes wide.

"Could be." Ray described the kid he'd seen.

"Don't recognize the description, but Cora and I are gone a lot lately." Mabel dabbed her mouth with a napkin. "I just can't believe it's a child."

"Me, either." Cora wagged her head. "Got to be a bad guy."

"Yes indeed," Mabel said. "A bad guy."

"Wasp spray," Cora murmured.

"Wasp spray?" Ray paused, fork in midair.

"Well, Faith doesn't have a man around to protect her. Wasp spray in the face is as good as anything to stop a derelict."

Ray winced. "You know this from experience?"

"Don't ask." Mabel shook her head. "Cora has been chasing men away her whole life. At least she lets that Tom Douglas sit next to her at church."

Cora harrumphed and blushed.

Faith giggled, lifted a fork of herbed potato chunks to her mouth, and her elbow brushed Ray's—again. "Sorry," Faith said. "Remember, I'm a lefty."

"Creative types." Cora dropped another slice of ham on her plate.

Ray glanced at Faith, smiling. "I'm not complaining, am I?"

"Uh-uh, he's not complaining, honey." Mabel emphasized her remark with a wag of her head. "So how's that pup, Faith?" Her attention switched to Ray. "You ought to go over to Faith's to check on your dog."

"He's not mine, Miss Mabel."

"We're going to post an ad in the *Bothell-Kenmore Reporter*. It comes out on Wednesday. We'll see if we can locate her rightful owner. If nobody responds within five days, we—"

"I'll be cleaning up poop," Cora finished and waved her hand.

"Not at the table, sister." Mabel cleared her throat. "Now Ray, tell Faith what happened to you in church."

Faith glanced sideways at her handsome friend. She read his reticence and opened her mouth to change the topic.

"The Lord spoke to him." Cora smiled sweetly. "Go on, tell Faith."

Ray released an audible sigh, and Faith had to hold back a laugh. Poor Ray. They treated him the same as when he was a teen.

"Okay," Ray started, "but I'm not exactly sure that the Lord was speaking to me. Pastor Gary said the church needed a full-time music minister. We prayed, and I felt. . ." He took a bite of bread, which Faith sensed was a diversionary tactic.

"Called," Mabel whispered solemnly. "He felt called. Oh well. Ray was always serenading the neighborhood with his guitar."

"Oh honey, and the music he wrote." Cora closed her eyes. "Heavenly."

Faith felt a push to intercede on his behalf. "Well but, he needs to be very sure." She thought of her own choices, her family's rebuff. "Some decisions are irreversible."

"Amen to that!" Cora fairly shouted. "If it's God, He'll be sure to confirm His wishes."

Ray continued to eat in silence when Mabel slapped the tabletop, giving Faith a jolt. "I almost forgot," Mabel said. "That Sally person called."

Faith's ears perked up. This time she had no desire to interrupt the sisters to rescue Ray's hide. *Who's Sally?* she wondered, and why did Ray look suddenly animated and interested? Was she the woman he'd referred to briefly during their walk?

"You mean *Bailey*? She called the house phone?" Ray yanked his cell from his belt and groaned. "I turned my phone off for the church service." He turned on the ringer and looked back up at Mabel. "When did she call?"

"About fifteen minutes after you went outside." Mabel started to hum.

"But I was right on the front porch." The frustration in his voice came through loud and clear.

"Prayin'," Cora said. "We wasn't about to interrupt your conversation with God for *her*."

Faith studied the peas on her plate, arranging them, she realized, into a smiley face.

"Okay, so, did Bailey leave a message?"

Gee, he was awfully anxious over a phone call from this Bailey person. Faith swirled the peas, messing up the happy smile, and shoveled them into her mouth.

"Said call her cell. She'll be around this afternoon." Mabel handed Faith a bowl of broccoli. "C'mon now, don't be shy."

"I couldn't." Faith held up her hand.

Ray stood, his chair scraping against the wooden floor. "Great lunch." He brought his plate to the sink, and Mabel and Cora took the opportunity to look at one another and roll their eyes. Faith pretended not to notice.

"Delicious." She stood, empty plate in hand. "I should be getting back. Sparkles needs attention."

"I'll walk you out," Ray offered.

Cora took the plate from her hand, and each sister gave her a hug. "You stop by any time, you hear?" Mabel returned to the sink, and Cora started clearing the table.

At the front door, Ray looked down into her face and tucked an errant piece of hair behind her ear. A fond gesture that she wouldn't allow just anyone to do.

"Listen, if we can't find Sparkles's owner, I want you to keep her. Just extra protection. . .just in case."

"Protection? That little—"

"Noisy dog. Yeah."

"Oh. She's a yapper, true enough."

His gaze had grown distant, and she watched him touch his cell phone. He wanted to call Bailey, whoever she was. Had to be that fiancée of his. Faith patted his arm, said good-bye, and walked down the stairs. She heard the click of the door behind her and suddenly felt vulnerable and sad.

As she entered her house she searched her mind for a reason for her weird emotions. Probably the broken fence. Any woman living alone would have good reason to worry about a potential intruder. But why did she feel sad?

She went to the crate in her bedroom. Sparkles whined as she unlocked it.

"You're adorable, and you're healing quickly." Faith picked her up and snuggled her against her shoulder like a baby. "If we can't find your owner, I'd be happy to keep you, little girl."

They headed for her kitchen, and she set the terrier on the floor where her bowl was filled with dry food. She then went to the fridge for a bottle of water. Four bottles on the shelf. She bent over and looked more closely. "That's odd. . ." She moved the container of milk. Just a couple of days ago she'd put six bottles in here, hadn't she? She shuffled other food items. Worry knotted her stomach. Was she losing her mind? Or had someone really come into her home? To steal water? It made no sense; therefore, she wouldn't make a fool of herself by telling Ray.

eight

Ray rolled over and took a deep, appreciative sniff of. . .bacon and coffee. His eyes flew open, and he looked at the clock that read 5:00 a.m. on Monday morning. First working day of the week and his first day back at the precinct.

Drifting up from the kitchen were Cora's and Mabel's voices, singing a Psalm in unison. Ray smiled as warm memories flooded his mind. Their heartfelt praises to God soothed his soul.

After a quick shower, he put on his uniform. Is this job what he really wanted to be doing? His thoughts turned to Sunday and the pastor's announcement about hiring a music minister. The desire to take the job had rattled him. He dismissed it from his thoughts as he left his room. No time to think about it right now.

The top step squeaked as he headed down the stairs, and he smiled. That squeak had been like an alarm when he spent weekends here as a young man. He'd had trouble sneaking downstairs without one of the sisters knowing he was up. Hard to take midnight trips to the refrigerator to sneak a snack. And the one time he'd tried to get out to meet a friend in the middle of the night was disastrous.

He paused at the door to the kitchen. Cora was putting bacon on a paper towel to drain. Mabel was at the table reading her Bible. His heart lurched as he realized again how much he loved the sisters.

"Smells wonderful!" Ray announced.

Mabel looked up, smiled, and patted the chair next to her. "Come and sit. You need a big breakfast before you go to work."

Ray slipped a finger into his belt. "Not sure I really need a big breakfast."

"Nonsense," Cora said as she put scrambled eggs on plates. "Sit. Eat."

Ray obeyed.

"You ask the blessing," Mabel told him.

He said a prayer of thanks and dug in. "Hmm, I've been away too long."

"I'll say." Mabel stabbed her Bible with her index finger. "I've got the perfect scripture verse for you today. Look here, Psalm 33:4–5, 'For the word of the Lord is right and true; he is faithful in all he does. The Lord loves righteousness and justice; the earth is full of his unfailing love.'"

"Amen," Cora called from her place at the stove.

Ray nodded. "Amen. I know He's faithful, ladies, and I'm going to need a large dose of His 'unfailing love' this morning. I may end up facing my nemesis."

Mabel set her Bible on the table and tilted her chin. "Now don't go putting all the blame on that other man for what that Sally did."

"*Bailey,* not Sally."

"Takes two to tango," Cora mumbled as she ambled to the table.

Mabel patted the Bible with her open hand. "We heard you on the phone last night, yakking. Was that Bailey?"

Ray had forgotten this part of staying with the sisters. They knew everything. "I can't see it's really anyone's business."

Cora clucked her tongue. "Boy wants privacy."

"Mm-hm," Mabel said. "Privacy? Nothing's private because God knows everything. And we're prayin' about this. It is the rest of your life, you know."

Her logic made sense in a weird way, not that he thought he didn't need privacy.

"You weren't laughing much when you were talking to her." Cora shook her head.

Mabel waved her hand. "No indeedy. Not like with Faith."

He inhaled, ready to argue, but realized he couldn't. Laughter came easily with Faith, but then they had known each other so long, and they didn't have any dark issues to overcome in their friendship.

Cora planted her hands on her hips and wagged her head. "Just look at you. Handsome thing, isn't he, sister?"

Ray was grateful for the change of topic. "Why thank you."

"We'll be praying for you today." Mabel patted his arm. "You're an officer of the law, and that's a godly thing, son. Remember, 'the Lord loves righteousness and justice.'"

"Right." Ray drew a deep breath. "That incident in church yesterday. . .must've been my overactive imagination. I've already got a full-time job."

"We're not saying that either." Cora held his face with her hands and looked in his eyes. "The Lord is faithful. He'll speak to you again on that matter. Got it?"

"Got it." Ray concentrated on his food, and the sisters chitchatted about people he didn't know.

After breakfast he took his plate to the sink and gave each of them a good-bye hug. "I'm off. Philip's going to pick me up so I can drive my patrol car home tonight."

They followed him to the front door with a laundry list of admonitions. "No more bad thoughts. . . . God is good *all* the time. . . . Don't let the devil steal your joy. . . ."

"Morning, bro!" Philip said when Ray climbed into the passenger seat, ears still ringing with the sisters' words.

"Hey." Ray glanced at Faith's house. Her truck wasn't in the driveway.

"You ready for this?" Philip asked, glancing over at him.

"I suppose I am."

"You sound less than thrilled."

Ray shrugged. "Nervous is more like it."

Philip cleared his throat. "I ran into Dwight at the courthouse. He has it in his head to apologize to you."

"Hmm." Ray held his tongue.

"I can imagine how you feel, knowing Dwight and knowing what he did to you, but hitting him again won't solve anything."

"I'll be fine," Ray said. "That will never happen again. With anyone." And he meant it.

For the rest of the drive, Philip updated Ray about the latest, and when he turned onto 101st Avenue, approaching the red brick building that housed the police department, Ray had relaxed. The tension he'd been feeling had mostly dissipated. That could be from distance, or, Ray hoped, God had done a work inside him. The brawl Ray had started with Dwight took place when he was off duty. To his surprise, Dwight, a lawyer, hadn't come after him. But Ray's chain of command had suggested a short leave to cool his heels.

One month in the Tri-Cities had led to a lengthy leave as the thought of seeing his ex-fiancée with Dwight set him afire with a fury he couldn't fight at first. But little by little, he mellowed. And when Philip phoned to say Dwight and Bailey had split, Ray made his final decision to return home. He had to see if reconciliation with Bailey was possible. And today, armed with the Word of God and Cora's and Mabel's prayers, he was also ready to face his enemy head-on.

When Ray and Philip walked into the building, the first person he saw was Bill Snyder.

"See you in briefing," Philip said and took off down the hall.

"Ray." Snyder came over, shook his hand, and slapped him on the back. "Good to see you, buddy." The older man had been a police officer for years, and he'd known Ray's father. Ray pumped his hand harder.

"You ready for this?" Snyder asked. "You know sooner or later you're going to see Dwight Connor again."

Ray nodded. "Yes, I'm ready."

"Remember, son, once you lose your cool, you can't get it back."

He nodded, knowing Snyder's words were true. He'd never forget that, having learned it the hard way.

Snyder gave Ray a thumbs-up. "Good to have you back."

Ray smiled and strode toward Captain Butler's office and tapped on the door.

"Come in."

He entered, and Captain Butler popped out of his chair, came around, and shook his hand. The tall man, built like a brick, scowled at Ray. That was his normal expression, and it had become etched into his features. "Everything is in order. On paper you're ready to start back, but. . ."

Butler pointed to the chair in front of his desk, and Ray sat. "Yeah, I'm ready."

Butler ran his hand over his buzz-cut, steel gray hair. "Think you can handle working around Connor? He's a public defender. You'll see him again. I don't want any trouble."

The mention of Dwight's name wasn't the hot poker to his heart that it used to be. Ray was surprised. "I'm okay."

Butler looked leery. "You're lucky Dwight didn't sue you. . . and us."

"That's true."

"If it happens again, I can't answer for your future."

"I understand, sir."

"You're one of the best we had, Reed." Butler rested his hands on his desk. "You and your brother. . .it's in your blood."

Ray digested the compliment in silence, wondering if this was confirmation from the Lord that he was to continue in law enforcement.

"Well, welcome back." Butler's mouth turned up, which was supposed to pass for a smile even though it just served to deepen his scowl. Ray had never heard Butler actually laugh.

He shook the captain's proffered hand. "Thanks again, sir."

Back in the hallway, Ray removed his jacket, and he heard two familiar voices behind him. He turned and saw Dwight standing next to Snyder, hands buried in his trouser pockets, rocking heel to toe. That cocky, arrogant air. . .

"Lord, I forgive." Still, Ray couldn't help but wonder. . . how did Dwight face himself in the mirror every day? But Connor had always been that way. Ray hadn't paid much attention until it affected him personally.

Connor turned his head and registered the sight of Ray. His jaw dropped open in mock surprise. His old, sarcastic humor. "Is that. . ." He left Snyder's side and took long strides across the tile floor, hand extended. "Welcome back, Ray."

Ray nodded and grasped Dwight's hand. "Thank you."

Their eyes met, then Dwight's gaze flickered.

"I hear you and Bailey called it quits." Ray blurted out the words before he could stop himself as he released Dwight's hand.

Connor looked up, then dropped his gaze to the floor. "Yeah, um, listen. About that. . ."

"I'm sorry, I shouldn't have said anything." Ray meant it.

"It's okay. It's all behind us now." Dwight met his gaze. "It really is."

Ray knew that was as close to an apology as he was going to get from Dwight, and it was enough. They nodded at each other. Ray walked away, testing his emotions. No anger. No more desire to lash out. The lack of hostility felt odd. Like he was light-headed. Ray shot a thanks to the Lord as he realized that what had happened more than a year ago no longer held him captive.

nine

Faith's intercom buzzed, and she frowned at the phone as she picked up the headset.

"Dr. Hart," Gladys said, "a man is here to see you. Um. . . his name is Ray."

"Ray is here?" Faith smiled. "I'll be right out."

She walked out into the front waiting area. Ray stood next to the counter. "Hey!" Warmth enveloped her at the sight of her friend.

"Hi. Sorry I didn't call. Just felt like I wanted to do something spur of the moment." Despite his smile of greeting, his eyes lacked their usual mischievous sparkle.

She resisted the temptation to reach out and touch his arm to comfort him. "Are you okay?"

She felt Gladys's stare and realized this was probably the first time she'd seen Faith with anyone besides clients and work staff.

Ray shrugged. "It's just been a strange day. Are you hungry? I haven't eaten yet, and I'm thinking of going to Canyons."

"I like that place." Faith considered her workload for half a beat, then decided everything could wait. As was their agreement, Debbie was handling the evening clients, and if she needed Faith, she could call her cell. Besides, Ray looked as though he could use a listening ear. "I'm game," she said with a smile.

"Good." Ray gave her a thumbs-up. "You don't mind riding on the back of my Harley with me, do you? I'll bring you back here after we're done so you can pick up your truck."

Ah, the mischievous sparkle was back, and she couldn't resist. "It's been a long time since I've been on a motorcycle. Well, really they were dirt bikes and never that big. . . ." Faith chewed her lower lip as she looked at the bike through the front window of the clinic. "Do you have a helmet for me?"

Gladys gasped, but Faith ignored her. Being shocked by Faith's unusual, spontaneous behavior would give her staff something to talk about.

"Sure do." Ray winked. "It's got to be less scary than basic training."

Faith laughed. "All right then. Give me a minute and I'll change."

She hurried to her office in the back where she kept a pair of everyday clothes in a small closet. She spent so many hours at the clinic she should just move in and save herself the monthly mortgage on her house. As she slipped into her jeans, her heart raced, surprising her. *This isn't a date!* Her excitement over having dinner with Ray was simply happiness about being with her friend again.

Faith emerged from her office and asked Gladys to tell Debbie she had gone to dinner. Outside, Ray offered her a dazzling smile. Her friend had certainly grown into a handsome man. She couldn't help but notice.

"I'm ready," she stated simply.

"Don't be scared. I'm a great driver, despite all the un-deserved comments I get from Mabel and Cora." Ray took the extra helmet from the back of his bike. "Let me put this on for you."

As he placed the helmet on her head, he tucked in loose strands of her hair. Her skin felt warm where his fingers brushed.

"Beautiful," Ray said.

Beautiful?

He grinned, hopped on his bike, and patted the black seat behind him. "C'mon, m'lady. Your steed awaits."

The picture of Sleeping Beauty riding with her prince on his horse flitted through her mind. *Silly!* Faith mounted the bike in one fast motion.

"Wrap your arms around my waist," Ray instructed.

She did as she was told, then closed her eyes and inhaled deeply. The scent of his leather jacket and the light fragrance of his cologne filled her senses. The rev of the engine made her open her eyes. She tightened her grip at his waist as he pulled away.

The warm wind blew over them, and Faith relaxed, savoring the experience. And for the first time in as long as she could remember, she relaxed. Ray still had that effect on her. Being with him was peaceful.

They reached Canyons in a few short minutes. Too short. She got off the bike slowly, pulled off the helmet, and said, "Thanks for that. I enjoyed it."

"Really?" Ray's smile warmed her heart. Something about him reminded her of a little boy in a man's body. She'd always felt that way about him, that childlike quality that she loved.

They were seated by a window and picked up their menus.

"You want some nachos?" Ray asked.

"Absolutely. And you know what I want for dinner?" She grinned at him. "Ribs."

"Me, too."

After they placed their order, Ray looked antsy.

"What is it, Ray?"

"I could use your advice, Faith."

He spoke her name with such sincerity it took her a second to find her voice. "Yes, right, how can I help?"

"A couple of things really. I need prayer for clear direction on this music ministry position that's opened up at Bothell Community."

"I'm a step ahead of you. After I heard of your experience in church yesterday, I went home and added the request to your name on my prayer list. I know God is faithful. He'll give you clear direction. It's a big step, leaving your present job."

"Yeah, it is," Ray admitted. "And there's something else."

The waiter arrived at their table with the nachos and drinks.

"Thanks," Ray said and took her hand. "Want to bless the food?"

Faith nodded and prayed, grateful that Ray was back in her life. He made her feel important and needed. When they said their amens, she swallowed past the lump in her throat and smiled.

"You were saying?"

Ray looked at her thoughtfully for a long moment. "I guess it's all right to ask a female friend for relationship advice, right?"

His words weren't what she expected and stung. She wasn't sure why. Faith made an exaggerated effort at nonchalance with a wave of her hand and a forced smile. "Of course. That's what friends are for. I can't promise you I'll be much help. The few romances I've had were short and sweet." Faith laughed. "Or not so sweet."

Ray finished chewing a mouthful of nachos and grimaced. "Well then, I'd say it was the guy's loss."

Sure it was, she thought. "No, I always focused on career. It was the Navy, then medical school, now it's making a go of the clinic."

"Me, too. Career first, and I'm pretty sure that's how I lost my fiancée."

"Fiancée, eh?" The food in her mouth turned to sawdust.

"Yes. I've got to catch you up on things."

They finished their nachos, and dinner arrived at the table before Ray's story was over. Faith's appetite diminished as Ray talked about Bailey. Overriding the mix of her emotions, anger was bubbling up inside her. She had no right to judge Bailey, but how could the woman have done that to Ray?

"You're such a good guy." Faith dropped her gaze to her plate and finished gnawing a sparerib. As much as she resented what she was about to say, she had to be honest with her friend. "Someone like you doesn't stop loving someone just because they're unfaithful. It's not your nature." His nature was the same as it had always been. Loving and committed.

Dark brows furrowed, Ray gave her an assessing look. "Are you sure you don't mind listening to me?"

Her heart paused as though she'd been caught in deceit. "No, why?"

"It's just that your face looks like you're in pain or something."

That was an accurate description of how she felt, and she wasn't sure why. She pushed her feelings aside. She was here for Ray.

"Not at all. I told you I was willing to listen, and I meant it."

Ray gave her another long look, then nodded. "So, thanks to Mabel and Cora, you already know that Bailey called. And I went ahead and called her back."

Faith swallowed a small bite of coleslaw, forcing her stomach to settle. "So, how'd that go?"

"She's in San Diego, visiting with her parents. We decided to have a talk when she's back in town."

"Hmm." Faith cleared her throat and took a sip of water while Ray looked at her expectantly.

"What?" they said simultaneously.

"Nothing," Faith said. "Just that you seem to have made up your mind already. You want to get back with her, don't you?"

Head tilted, Ray's eyes narrowed. Had animosity come through in her voice? She was not good at disguising her feelings, and her mind raced to come up with a justification.

"I'm just saying. . ." What was she saying? "You—you sort of asked for my input, but you intend to go back with. . ." She couldn't bear to say her name. Worse, she sounded like a woman scorned.

Ray smiled. "You sound a bit like Mabel and Cora."

"I do?"

"Protective. I like that, even though from them it can be overkill."

She sighed with relief.

"So tell me what you think."

"I don't like the idea that Bailey cheated on you, Ray. If she felt you spent too much time at work, she should've given you fair warning." She flicked back her hair and looked him in the eye, feeling the strength of her convictions to her toes.

"But in all fairness, I might be the wrong one to ask. I'm personalizing because—"

"It's fine. Most people would feel as you do. Cora and Mabel. . .they have very strong opinions about Bailey—or as Mabel calls her, Sally. My brother"—Ray inhaled deeply—"he's called me a fool more than once."

She wouldn't go so far as to agree with Philip out loud, but the temptation was there.

Ray tapped her plate. "You aren't eating. I'm sorry. I'm spreading a dark cloud. Let's forget romance for the rest of the night and concentrate on friendship and fun."

"Friendship and fun," she echoed. "Sounds good." She began nibbling on a rib to make the effort, but her appetite had fled.

He was as good as his word. He regaled her with stories from work, and soon she relaxed, but in the back of her mind, she couldn't let go of the fear that he would restore his relationship with Bailey. She was worried for him. No, it was more than that, but what? She watched his animated expression as he told her about the weird man he'd stopped who thought the speeding ticket Ray gave him was a raffle ticket. She'd always loved the way Ray's eyes crinkled when he laughed. A sudden gnawing fear of losing him again came over her. She knew most women weren't keen on their men having female best friends. She didn't like the picture in her head of Bailey whispering in Ray's ear to stop seeing her. She gripped her napkin in her lap as it occurred to her that her feelings seemed an awful lot like jealousy.

ten

"Yo, Ray-mond!"

Ray was leaving the precinct and turned at the sound of his brother's voice. "Hey, Philip."

"What's shakin' today? It's a great day. Fri-day." Philip slapped Ray's shoulder. "You been rounding up bad guys left and right?"

Ray smiled. "Nope. Not really. Just routine stuff. What about you?"

"You know that gas station robbery last week?"

"Yeah." Ray had heard about it in a briefing on his first morning back at work. "Anything new in the case?"

Philip shook his head. "We have suspects, but can't prove anything. I'm just hoping the gas station attendant will come out of his coma."

"What about security cameras?"

"Security cameras weren't working." Philip shook his head. "Why people don't take advantage of technology, I don't know."

They began walking together. "You got plans this weekend?" Philip asked.

Ray hesitated and shrugged. "Not sure."

"How's it going with Bailey?"

Ray shrugged again. "Haven't seen her yet, if that's what you mean. We've talked on the phone."

"I see," Philip said softly. "You're a better man than me."

"What does that mean?"

"If a woman did to me what she did to you? It'd be over. Period. No talking. No nothing."

"But what if it was your fault?"

"Was it really *all* your fault, Ray? Do you know that for sure, or is that what she said to excuse her behavior?"

Ray felt himself growing angry at Philip and reined in his

temper. He searched his mind for another topic—one that wouldn't bring such a negative reaction.

"You remember Faith Hart?" Ray blurted.

"Little Faith Hart." Philip grinned. "Of course I remember her. Nice girl. You two were glued at the hip every summer when you were teens." Philip jabbed Ray with his elbow. "She's back in town, you know. In fact, she's living next to Mabel and Cora. I ran into Cora one day, and she told me. You must have seen her."

"I have."

"And?"

"And what?" Ray glanced at his big brother suspiciously. What was he trying to say?

"And, did you talk? Is she nice-looking?"

Ray shook his head. "You're impossible. Don't you see women any other way but 'good-looking' or 'bad-looking'? Yes, we've talked. And, yes. She's nice-looking. She always has been."

"I see," Philip said again as they reached Ray's car. Philip tugged at his uniform collar. "You're wrong, you know."

"About what?"

"How I see women." Philip jingled change in his pocket.

Ray met his gaze. "Really?"

"Yes—at least in this case. It's more how I see people. Actions speak louder than words."

Ray frowned. "Are you being deliberately obtuse?"

"Nope. Just wanting everything to be okay with my little brother." Philip grinned. "I think it is."

"What does that mean?"

Philip laughed. "Exactly what I said. Besides, you got Mabel and Cora on your side. I might not be a religious man, but I sure am glad to know they're praying for us."

They exchanged good-byes, and by the time he reached the house, he'd stopped trying to figure out what Philip had meant. He looked over at Faith's house. No truck. She wasn't home yet. He felt disappointed. It would have been nice to talk to her. He climbed from the car, walked to the porch, and hesitated. What kind of hullabaloo was going on inside? He opened the door, and praise music spilled into the street. In the living room, Mabel and Cora were dancing, a sort of tarantella routine—arms locked and going in circular motions.

They both looked up at him, smiling. "We closed on the Victorian!" Mabel shouted over the din.

"Hey, great news." Ray closed the door and draped an arm around each sister. "Cause to celebrate, for sure."

Cora hit the OFF switch on the CD player, fanned herself, and motioned him to the kitchen table. "Yow-wee, Lordy, Lordy! He sure is good to us."

"And look what we have," Mabel said. "The original plans to the house. Why don't you look at them while I go finish fixin' dinner."

"I'm not real hungry," Ray said.

"Nonsense." Mabel spread the plans out on the coffee table. "You need to keep up your strength if you're going to help us with this project."

He and Mabel began studying the original plans to the historic home, and Ray began to share the sisters' excitement. "I can restore this beauty to what she used to be."

"Yes, indeed." Mabel patted his hand. "You always were creative. We would've never trusted anybody else with this work."

Ray's cell phone rang, and he took it from his belt. "Hello?" He sat back on the couch while Mabel pretended not to listen.

"Ray, this is Pastor Gary."

"Hey, Pastor. How can I help you?"

Mabel eyeballed him, and Ray shrugged in response.

"Two things, brother. Do you think you can fill in playing the guitar for us this Sunday? Um, actually, could you lead the worship?"

"Um, I'd be happy to do that, but I'm a little rusty with the songs."

"Huh-uh, the Lord is great and worthy to be praised," Mabel said.

Ray held his finger to his lips, but she just grinned.

"That brings me to my next question," Pastor Gary said. "Would you be willing to attend practice this evening? The worship team practices at seven."

Ray's heart sang with a joy that surprised him. "Absolutely. It would be my honor. I'll be there tonight."

Mabel hummed "Amazing Grace."

Ray hung up, smiling. "I guess you heard. I'm playing my guitar on Sunday."

"Yes indeed." Mabel turned her face toward the kitchen. "Cora? Ray is playing for the service this Sunday."

"Praise the Lord!" Cora hollered from the kitchen.

Good smells wafted into the living room, and Ray felt his appetite return.

"Oh," Mabel said as she stared at the house plan, "did we tell you we invited Faith to dinner tonight?"

ॐ

Faith pulled into her driveway, put the truck in PARK, and rubbed her tired eyes. As much as she looked forward to dinner with the sisters, and was eager to see Ray again, a part of her wanted to skip dinner, curl up on the sofa with Sparkles, and catch some z's. She sighed. Unfortunately she'd agreed to meet a client for late dessert. Okay, who was she trying to fool? She'd agreed to a date. But now she regretted the impulsive decision. Why had she done it, anyway?

Faith took her keys out of the ignition and caught movement through her rearview mirror. "That little kid again," she whispered. The girl stood beside Faith's front hedges, peering at her. Faith grabbed the handle of the car door, intent on speaking to her. As soon as she stepped foot out of the car, the freckle-faced youngster took off running down the road.

"Hey!" Faith called out. "Don't be scared."

Too late. She watched the girl's retreating form until she rounded the bend. Who was she, and what could she possibly want? She uttered a silent prayer for the youngster's safety before going inside her house.

Sparkles, more hyper than usual, was jumping and whining like crazy. Faith took her out of the crate, gave her plenty of attention, then took her for a walk. "You're in good shape," she said as she watched the dog hop up the front steps to her door. "You're healing well. And I'm going to leave you out of the crate this time." Despite the safety of daylight, an odd feeling washed over her—as if she was being watched.

છ

As soon as she entered the sisters' house, the two women and Ray came out of the kitchen to greet her.

"Good news," Cora said, and Mabel added, "Oh, lots of good news today. Come on in."

Ray stood smiling down at her and winked. "Nice to see you, Faith."

Her gaze latched onto his for a few beats too long, and a giggle bubbled out of her mouth. Awful! She never giggled. Mabel and Cora disappeared back into the kitchen, and the way Ray approached, she almost expected him to give her a welcoming hug.

"Nice to see you, too," she said.

"Come in." He tilted his head toward the kitchen, and Faith followed.

Mabel lined up the ladder-back chairs very close together, then instructed Ray and her to "sit right down," and quickly asked, "How's that precious little dog?"

"Um. . ." Aware that she and Ray were practically glued at the hip, Faith finally managed to find her voice. "Sparkles? Oh, she's doing great."

Ray nudged her with his elbow. "You should be on my other side, lefty."

"Cora says I'm artistic," she whispered, and Ray laughed and nudged her again.

"Have you put an ad in the 'Lost and Found' yet?"

"Yes, this morning. I wanted to first be sure Sparkles was

going to totally recover."

"I sure hope nobody abused that baby girl," Cora said, and Mabel came to sit beside her at the table, nodding.

The thought of abusive owners had occurred to her numerous times. She looked down at the stew Cora set before her. "Oh, this smells and looks divine."

Mabel said a prayer of thanks, and as they ate, the sisters relayed their good news about closing on the Victorian.

"The scalloped siding on the Victorian makes it look like a dollhouse," Faith said. But she loved the house she was sitting in even more. "Will you sell this one then?"

"Yes. . ." Tears gathered in Mabel's eyes. "I don't want to think about strangers living here. Ralphie carried me over the threshold in this house." Her gaze scanned the kitchen as if she were seeing it for the first time, and Faith found herself holding back tears. "We scraped together every cent we had to buy this place." She shrugged. "Oh well. God's got something new for us." She turned to Cora. "Right, sis?"

"Yes, He does." Cora patted Mabel's shoulder. "We've been praying that God brings the right people along who'll fill this house with love."

Mabel laughed through her tears. "Oh my. He's gonna bring along the perfect couple. He told me so."

"Here, here." Ray raised his glass of iced tea in agreement. "If I could afford it I'd buy it myself."

"You never know." Cora looked directly at Faith, and she didn't know what to make of it.

Ray elbowed Faith. "So what are you doing tonight?"

His question, sudden and out of left field, rendered her mute for a moment. She had nothing to feel awkward about, yet she dreaded having to respond. "I have a date."

"A date?" Mabel's eyes grew wide as saucers.

"You're going out?" Cora chimed in. "With a man?"

Faith laughed despite her discomfort, but she avoided Ray's eyes. "I think a date for me would be defined as going out with a man."

Mabel and Cora exchanged curious glances, and Faith turned to Ray for rescue. He was frowning, and her defenses went up.

"The guy works down the street from me as an accountant. He brought his dog in one day. . . ." What was she doing justifying her motives? "What am I supposed to do? Just work all the time? It's Friday night. The start of a weekend. Most people do fun stuff on Friday night." *Is that why I did this?*

"Well, I would think you'd want to spend more time with Ray." Cora's chin tilted. "You're just getting reacquainted again."

"Hmm, and after all those years apart." Mabel sighed. "A shame."

Speak up, Ray! Faith looked at him again. "He has a life of his own, don't you, Ray?"

"Not really." His frown had disappeared, and the mischievous smile that took its place told her he was going to play this for all it was worth. "Other than music practice tonight"—Ray clasped his fingers—"I usually come home after work and basically twiddle my thumbs." He demonstrated with exaggerated motions.

"Hmph." Mabel stood, and Cora followed her to the counter. "Go on and joke." She nudged Cora. "Before you know it they'll be forty and—"

"Home alone twiddlin' their thumbs."

Faith and Ray exchanged another glance. This time Ray was laughing.

"I'll get you back for this," Faith whispered.

eleven

Faith sat stiff with nerves between Cora and Mabel while Pastor Gary made the Sunday morning announcements. This was Ray's big day. Playing guitar with the worship team. She continued to pray silently for the Lord to anoint his heart, his hands. What would Ray do if he felt the call to full-time music ministry? Scary, but exciting. Her heart thumped hard. She'd been there and back with career choices. Was there ever a right or easy choice—something that would please all the people one loved?

"We have a special treat," Pastor Gary said. "Our brother, Ray Reed, is joining the worship team to help us this morning."

The loudest and longest applause came from Mabel and Cora. Their eyes shone like two proud mamas', fussing over their boy. Sweet, unconditional love. Cora dabbed a tear from the corner of her eye.

Smiling, and with a nod of appreciation, Ray settled on a stool behind the mic and nodded at the other musicians. Then he adjusted his guitar and closed his eyes. After whispering a prayer, he strummed some introductory chords. The other musicians began to play. As his raspy tenor proclaimed the goodness and faithfulness of God and as the instrument in his deft hands sang its own praises, tears sprang to Faith's eyes.

Thank You, Lord, for the gift of music You've given Ray. And now he was giving back the gift, blessing the congregation. Was this Ray's call? Could he walk away from the precinct and not look back? Would he feel regret?

After the worship time ended, silence fell over the congregation. It was as though all were as caught up as she. Faith drew a breath and wiped the tears off her cheeks with a hankie Cora had passed to her.

She stared at Ray. Beautiful inside and out. What if she'd answered his letters so many years ago? Faith watched him walk off the platform, then looked away. Why that thought now? Was she seeing Ray as potentially more than a friend? After all this time. She clasped the hankie in her hands and stroked the soft cloth with her fingertips. Nothing good could come of torturing herself with "what-ifs." She was what she always had been. Unromantic and single-mindedly focused on her goals. Besides, Ray was a man on a mission, intent on getting his fiancée back.

⌘

"That was lovely," Cora said from the backseat of the Thunderbird.

Ray turned the key, and the car roared to life.

"A God-given talent." Mabel sat beside her sister, then resumed humming a hymn.

"Anointed," Faith whispered.

Ray felt warmed by the compliments and looked over at Faith, sitting beside him in the passenger seat. "I was surprised how right it felt. It all just flowed. I can't describe it. Now I'm confused."

"I understand." Faith tucked her dark, long hair behind her ear. A nervous habit he found charming. "Maybe you can do both, Ray? Play on weekends for the church and still keep your job."

"Yeah, I could play, but not lead." Ray headed east toward home. "Pastor Gary really needs a full-time music minister. A staff member. Someone to help lead the flock in more than music."

"Pray on it," the sisters said simultaneously from the back. "Pray without ceasing," Cora added.

Their plain talk chased away some of his worry, and he laughed along with Faith.

"Didn't you pray on it, Ray?" Faith grinned.

He looked at her, and understanding dawned. Okay, this was payback because he went along with Cora and Mabel when they told Faith to spend more time with him. "Yes, I did." Ray frowned. "By the way, how'd your date go?"

Faith narrowed her eyes and looked like she wanted to give him a swift kick. "Wonderful! Thank you very much."

"Waste of time," Mabel said, "if you ask me."

"What's that, Miss Mabel?" Ray deadpanned.

"You two, fussin' around with this one and that one. . ." Mabel muttered something inaudible under her breath.

"This one and that one?" Faith glared at Ray. "It was only one date, Miss Mabel. One. It's not like I've dated every single guy in town."

Ray pulled into the driveway. He could see a red stain working up Faith's cheeks. Her temper. Enough teasing for one day. Time for a change of topic. "Do you have the materials to finish your fence? We can do that before lunch."

"Yes. I picked them up this week. Sounds good to me." Faith's face was still red. "I'll go change."

Cora exited the car on a grunt. "Uh-huh, you two need to be mending fences."

"Yes indeedy," Mabel agreed. "Mending fences."

❧

Faith manned the staple gun as Ray held the wire in place.

"No sign of more break-ins?" Ray asked.

Faith considered the odd feelings she'd had and dismissed them. "Things have been calm, but you know, I'm still seeing that red-haired kid around. Maybe it was her messing around and she's stopped."

Ray sat back. "I saw her again, too."

Faith leaned into the staple gun.

"You're pretty handy with that," he noted.

"Learned to do a lot when my dad was out to sea," Faith murmured.

"Do you talk to him much?"

"I try to avoid him."

His eyes flashed surprise. "Oh."

And his one word spoke volumes. "You don't agree with that?"

He shrugged. "I didn't say that. It's just that. . ."

"What?" Faith felt her temper rising.

"Nothing. It's none of my business. Your face is getting red. I don't want to get yelled at."

She sat back and waited for Ray to stretch more chicken wire over the fence. "You know me too well. And you're right. I don't want to talk about my father. But at least because of him I'm not a sissy."

"Very true. You're definitely not a girlie girl." Ray held the wire.

"So what does that mean?" She jammed the staple gun against the wire fencing and pushed the trigger.

He looked her in the eye. "I didn't mean that in a bad way, just that you can hold your own with the best of them. No offense."

"None taken." Faith shrugged and kept working. "So, is Bailey a 'girlie girl'?"

"Hmm, good question." Ray blew out a long breath and stared off into the distance. "I guess you could say"—he frowned—"she's petite. Feminine." He laughed. "Maybe a diva."

Of course. Faith forced a short laugh. "I guess we're done here." She stood. "Hey, so when's the big day?"

Ray frowned. "Meaning?"

"Your face-to-face meeting with Bailey?" She cleared her throat. Her voice was definitely an octave too high and rang with false cheer. She was feeling a bit hostile toward the feminine girlie diva. The fact that her feelings seemed a bit like jealousy made things worse.

"Oh that." Ray leaned against a fence post. "This coming Wednesday. I don't know what to expect. Haven't seen her in over a year."

A bolt of unpleasant emotion shot through her. Anger? Why should she be angry? "Well I hope you're not nervous or anything." Faith wiped her hands on a rag. "She's lucky you'd consider going back with her. Some men wouldn't. . ." She let her voice trail off as heat rose from her neck to her face.

"Hey." Ray took her hands in his. "If I didn't know better, I'd think you were—"

"Jealous? Well, I'm not."

"No. That's not what I was about to say."

Head tilted, Ray peered at her closely, and her stomach did a backflip. What had gotten into her? She had survived four years in the Navy, vet school, and opening a clinic, and suddenly she was an emotional wreck!

"I was just going to say that it was like the old days, when, God forbid, anybody breathed a word against me, you'd come to my defense."

Faith felt her shoulders relax. He'd given her an out. "Yeah, I guess old habits die hard."

"Lunch is ready," Mabel called from the porch.

With a wave, Faith acknowledged that they'd heard. "Be right in."

Faith put the leftover fencing and staple gun on her back porch. They walked together in silence to the back door. She wanted to say so much to him, but no words would come. What could she say when she was unable to sort her own scrambled emotions?

twelve

Ray got in from work, dropped his keys on the table in the foyer, then glanced at the grandfather clock in the living room. He had forty minutes before Bailey would show—if she showed. She said she'd try, if her boss didn't keep the advertising crew late.

Mabel walked down the hall holding the plans for the Victorian.

"I'd like to look at those," he said. "I'm always fascinated by old plans. Be interesting to see if any structural changes were made to the interior."

"And we'd like you to." She hovered a few feet from him. "You gonna take off your gun? Makes me nervous."

"You've got that hunting rifle of Ralph's hanging up in his old office. Why would mine be any different?"

Mabel planted her hands on her hips. "Don't you be mouthy with me, young man. Yours is loaded. Mine has no bullets, lucky for you."

Ray grinned. "Yes, ma'am. I'll go change now."

Mabel swatted his arm. "I'll take these to the kitchen while you get out of that uniform."

"Really amazing that you've got the original blueprints," Ray murmured. He couldn't wait to study them more closely and reluctantly went to his bedroom to shower and change.

He dressed in haste, hurried downstairs, then joined the sisters at the table.

"You going to Wednesday service with us tonight?" Mabel asked.

Aha, he forgot they'd be out of the house this evening. Relief washed through him. "Can't make it tonight."

The sisters exchanged glances, but voiced no objections.

Odd. He felt a bit sneaky not telling them he'd made a date to see Bailey. He figured they'd find out once she got here but wanted to avoid a sermon beforehand. Bad enough he'd gotten a strange reaction when he'd told Faith about his ex.

A clap of thunder shook the house, and Mabel let loose an earsplitting hoot. "Lord, have mercy!"

Hand on her heart, Cora shuddered. "Lord, help us all." She got up, went to the kitchen window, and parted the sheer curtains. "I'm not driving in this downpour, I can tell you that."

Ray watched hopefully for Mabel's reaction. Maybe she'd disagree with Cora. A private conversation with Bailey would be nearly impossible with the sisters home.

"Uh-huh, no sense taking any chances," Mabel concurred and looked across the table. "Well, you've got us for company tonight, son."

"You want some blueberry buckle with ice cream?" Cora asked.

Ray groaned, but didn't say no.

After dessert they cleaned up the dishes, and the sisters said they wanted to get back to the blueprints.

Ray looked at his watch. "Maybe it can wait till tomorrow?"

"Huh?" Mabel scowled. "A minute ago you couldn't wait to look at them. Now you want to wait? You feelin' okay? You're acting strange tonight. Sort of nervous."

"Come sit with us." Cora strode into the living room and Ray followed, Mabel on his heels.

He was probably better off occupying his mind with house plans while he waited for Bailey to show. He should tell them now about her visit, but what if she didn't come? He'd endure a good "dressing down," as the sisters would put it, and for no reason.

They poured over the Victorian house plans, with Cora and Mabel strongly voicing their ideas about decorating style and color.

The doorbell rang, and Cora popped off the sofa. "I'll get it."

Ray got to his feet. "No, I will."

"Sit!" Cora commanded. "You two keep studying that blueprint. Maybe it's Faith."

It would be nice to see Faith again. But he knew better, and the familiar voice at the door confirmed it was Bailey. He felt a surge of nervousness.

"Who is that?" Mabel called out.

Ray got to his feet again. "Excuse me. We'll get back to this later."

"Bailey is here to see Ray," Cora announced from the front hallway. "You can put your umbrella here," he heard her tell Bailey. "My lands, you'll catch a chill in this weather and with no sleeves."

"Bailey? Is calling on you?" Mabel whispered. "In my day women waited for the man to do the—"

"Miss Mabel," Ray warned as Bailey and Cora walked into the room.

Bailey was still beautiful, but her waist-length hair now barely grazed her bare shoulders.

"Ray." Bailey approached with a smile, and he was surprised by how awkward he felt. He reached out to hug her, and she held him tighter and longer than was comfortable, considering their audience. Ray stepped out of her embrace, feeling the stares of the sisters.

"Ohh, honey," Mabel said to Cora. "It's time to take out our Bibles."

"I'll say. We'll have church right here and now." Head held high, Cora sashayed out of the room behind her sister, muttering, "Lord, help us all."

Already they were starting up. Ray pointed to the sofa. "Have a seat, will you?" He was about to apologize for the lack of privacy, but Bailey looked bubbly and happy and didn't seem to care.

"So," they said simultaneously, and Bailey laughed.

"It's great to see you, Ray." She squeezed his forearm. "You're looking better than ever." She searched his eyes, dropped her gaze, and blew out a long breath. "I'm sorry."

Cora's voice traveled from the kitchen. . .something about "binding spirits and loosing the power of God."

Bailey glanced in the direction of the kitchen. "They're really serious about the Bible."

Ray just shrugged. "They missed their Wednesday night Bible study, so they're doing their devotions here instead."

"Whatever. I don't care what anyone else is doing. I'm here to see you." Bailey slipped her slender hand into his. "I don't know how to tell you how sorry I am."

Ray felt oddly ill at ease. He'd waited more than a year to hear her say those words, and now that she was here, next to him, he wasn't sure how he felt.

"I don't know how else to explain it. . . . I guess I fell under Dwight's spell." Her watery gaze softened his heart. *Forgive.* He had to learn to be more forgiving.

"You were the best thing that ever happened to me, Ray."

Then why? he wanted to ask, but Bailey sniffled and continued, "I want back what we had."

"No," Ray heard himself say. "No, you don't want what we had. You weren't happy with what we had. You want—"

"I was selfish. I wanted more attention from you. Too much attention."

"And that's where Dwight came in, huh? He gave you what I couldn't?" Ray drew a breath. It hurt to think of the two of them together. Would it always hurt this badly? "I know I'm far from perfect, but. . ." The validity of Faith's words came back to him. "You could've given me fair warning."

"I was afraid to," she whispered. "Afraid to pressure you."

"Truth, Lord." Cora's voice rose in prayer. "Reveal all truth."

Bailey inhaled and glanced over her shoulder. "I think they hate me."

"Who?" Ray pulled back and looked down into her face, and Bailey hitched her thumb toward the kitchen.

"Impossible," Ray whispered. "They don't hate anybody." He pondered her answer to his question. Afraid to pressure him? Was it that simple? And if it were, would it happen again? This wasn't the time nor place for a deep discussion on the topic, especially since he wasn't sure what questions to ask or what to say. "So, you still go to church?"

Bailey sighed. "Not every Sunday. I went to your church a couple times after you left town, but I felt judged. Tried church hopping for a while. Whatever. I guess I became disenchanted."

Disenchanted. Like she'd become with him? Ray inched away on the sofa cushion, putting distance between them. He needed to think clearly. Impossible while he inhaled Bailey's perfume and shampooed hair.

"Are you involved with anybody else?" Bailey held up her hands. "I wouldn't blame you if—"

"No," Ray stated flatly, discounting his friendship with Faith.

Her lips curved in a glossy smile. "Good. That's good."

The doorbell rang, and Ray scowled. "I wonder who—"

"God is good." Mabel bustled past the living room entrance and headed for the door.

"Can we start seeing each other again?" Bailey's words rushed out of her mouth, and she clutched his hand.

Yes, he thought, but the word wouldn't come. Isn't this what he'd been looking forward to, wishing for? "I think it'll take some time for me—"

"It's Faith," Mabel called out.

"Did you hear that?" Cora dashed into the living room. "It's *Faith* at the front door."

"Yes, I couldn't help but hear that *Faith is here,*" Ray growled, and the sounds of steps coming down the hall told him she and Mabel were headed his way.

"Don't you be a smart mouth," Cora said, swatting his arm on the way to the front door.

"Who's *Faith*?" Bailey mimicked Cora's voice.

"The next-door neighbor, and it so happens, an old friend of mine."

Bailey narrowed her eyes.

"A friend of Mabel's and Cora's, too," he amended.

"I don't want to interrupt him if he has company," Faith protested.

"No bother, honey." Mabel's voice was firm and reassuring. "Go on into the living room."

"None at all," Cora agreed. "You need a police officer; Ray is a police officer."

"Indeed he is," Mabel said. "Handy to have one around when you need one, that's what I say."

Ray came to attention as the three entered the living room, Mabel practically pushing Faith. She was wet and pale and carried Sparkles in her arms.

He slipped his hand from Bailey's and stood. "What's wrong? Did something happen?"

"Someone's been on my back porch again." Faith switched her gaze to the sofa, and her eyes grew wide. "Oh, is this a bad time?"

"No," Ray assured as Bailey approached and echoed, "No."

An awkward moment of silence ensued.

"Since nobody's going to introduce me,"—Bailey gave Ray a sideways glance, then stuck out her hand—"I'm Bailey Cummings."

"Oh, right." Faith shook her hand. "Nice to meet you. I've heard a lot about you."

"Good, I hope." Bailey glanced at Ray and then the sisters. "So you're the next-door neighbor Ray was telling me about. Cute dog."

The sisters were silent, arms crossed. Not like them at all. He hadn't exactly referred to Faith as merely a neighbor, but a friend.

Mabel cleared her throat.

Ray faced Bailey. "I need to go check out Faith's place."

Bailey's eyes narrowed again, but she quickly recovered with a smile. "Want me to come, too?"

"Oh no, darlin'," Mabel said. "Too dangerous. We'll keep you company while Ray's gone."

"We will," Cora added. "We need to get to know you, anyway."

Bailey looked like she wanted to run.

"I'll be right back," Ray promised.

"Take your time," Mabel said with a distinct smile in her voice.

❦

So that was Ray's fiancée. *Ex-fiancée,* Faith amended. They didn't look like a match, but Faith had no intention of sticking her nose into his business again. As she walked across the yard with Ray, the wet lawn further soaked her slippered feet. A shiver raced up her spine, and she shuddered.

"You're cold." Ray slipped his arm around her shoulder.

She felt protected in his embrace and quickly reminded herself that Bailey was waiting for him inside. "I'm okay. I shouldn't have run out without my shoes, but I was scared." Sparkles whined. "Hush, little girl," Faith said, kissing the dog's head.

They went straight to the back porch, and Ray examined the door. "Looks like it was forced open. We'll have to fix this."

Faith set Sparkles down to allow the dog to relieve herself, and the little dog ran the perimeter of the yard. Ray smiled. "She's doing well."

"Yes, but it scares me that she was here alone when someone was inside."

When Sparkles was done, Faith dried her off with a towel she had for that purpose on the porch. Then she scooped her up.

They walked into the house, and she put Sparkles down. The dog immediately ran to the door and whined again. "Silly girl."

"Anything missing?" Frowning, Ray glanced around.

"I didn't stay long enough to have a close look." She sighed. "Would you like a soda?"

"No thanks." Ray followed her into the kitchen.

"Well, I need a bottle of water." Faith went to the refrigerator and rummaged around. Her heart sank. "Wait a sec. . . ." She moved aside a gallon of orange juice. "I'm going to sound nutty, but my cold cuts are gone."

"What?" He peered over her shoulder into the fridge. "Not nutty, but that's very odd."

"I wonder. . . ," she murmured. "Nothing of great value is ever missing. I wonder if that little girl is breaking in and taking food." Faith grabbed a bottle of water and slammed the fridge door closed. "This is giving me the creeps, even while I feel sorry for the kid."

"Hey." Ray placed his strong hands on her arms and looked down into her face. "I don't want you to worry. I'm right next door. But if you're home and you hear anything, dial 911 then call me. Okay?"

She nodded.

"I'll make another suspicious activity report. And I'll talk to my supervisor tomorrow and see if I can get permission to look into this further."

Please don't leave. Why was she feeling so desperate? Faith made a valiant effort at a smile. Was she really scared? Or did she just want to be with him? "I'm sorry to have disturbed you tonight. I didn't remember you had a date with your ex, er, Bailey."

A line formed between his dark brows, and he dropped his hands to his sides and shrugged. "Bailey. Not a date really. We needed to talk, but with Cora and Mabel at home—"

"Oh." Faith grimaced. She'd sensed right off that the sisters weren't happy Bailey was there. "I guess you'll be dating again." She felt her smile slipping.

Ray sighed. "I'm working on forgiveness. I believe in second chances."

She heard the "but" in his words. Anger rose up inside her and heated her face as she thought about what Bailey had done to him. "Well, just be careful. . ." *Or she'll walk all over you again.*

"Right. And you lock up after I leave."

With her heart heavy, she walked with Ray through the house to the front door. "Thanks for everything."

He stepped outside. "Anytime, Faith." Halfway across the lawn he stopped and turned. "Remember to call me if you need anything."

Tears pinched the backs of her eyes, but she nodded and tried to smile. She went back into the house, scolding herself for being such a wimp. She'd been happy living alone, feeling she lacked nothing. She prided herself for needing no one. When had the needy little girl surfaced? And why?

"Come on, Sparkles." The little dog followed her to her bedroom. Faith went to the window, lifted the blind slat, and peered across at Cora and Mabel's house. There, on the porch, Bailey stood looking up into Ray's face. Faith felt like a voyeur, watching what looked like an intense exchange between the two, but she was riveted to the spot, praying for the Lord to protect Ray.

Bailey reached up and slipped her arms around Ray's neck. They were about to kiss. She let the blind slat fall into place. She couldn't bear to look.

thirteen

Ray pulled his car into the driveway. He'd have to talk to Faith tonight, tell her his supervisor had given him permission to look into the break-ins even though they weren't going to file an official report yet. He cut the engine just as Mabel was walking to the garage with a briefcase that had belonged to Ralphie. It was the color of an old saddle with scars from years of use. He got off his bike and pointed. "Business?"

"Uh-huh." Mabel ran her hand over the bag. "Cora and I are meeting with our accountant to discuss the bed-and-breakfast. We left a plate for you in the refrigerator."

"Thank you," Ray said. "And I checked your oil this morning. That old Thunderbird burns it up."

"Yes, that's what Dilbert at the gas station says." She adjusted the feathered hat on her head and looked at the house. "Now, where is that sister of mine? She's as slow as molasses in winter."

"What time do you have to be at the accountant's, Miss Mabel?"

"Seven." She tapped her foot and clucked her tongue.

Ray bit back a grin. "How long does it take to get there?"

"Twenty minutes. . .with no traffic."

The front door opened and Cora stepped onto the porch and pulled the door shut. Ray glanced at his watch. Quarter after six. He flashed Mabel a grin. "Seems to me she's right on time. You're early."

Mabel pursed her lips. "You watch it, young man, or you'll find yourself scrubbing the kitchen floor on your hands and knees. You know as well as I do that the early bird gets the worm."

Ray laughed and hugged her. "You're so easy to tease."

84

She slapped his arm. "Shame on you." But she was smiling.

Cora trundled into the garage, black handbag slung over her arm. "You got a message from that. . .Bailey." Cora sniffed. "Said she tried your cell but the mailbox was full. She'll be free on Saturday."

Mabel's head whipped toward him as if she had been slapped. "Ray Reed! You're really going out with her? After what she did to you?"

"Yes, I'm going out with her." Annoyance made him snap.

Cora shook her head and opened the car door. "Mark my words, if she did it once, she'll do it again."

"A leopard doesn't change its spots," Mabel intoned, slipping behind the steering wheel.

They were both voicing his deepest fear—that he'd give Bailey another chance and she'd drop him again. Worry wormed its way into his heart.

Mabel held her hand out the car window, wiggling her index finger. "Come here."

He obeyed as he always did. She snatched his hand and held it. "You're a good boy, Ray. You like to believe the best in people, which is why police work wears you down. And why you get disappointed."

Ray patted her hand. "Don't you worry. My ears and eyes are open this time."

As they backed out of the driveway, Cora wagged her head. "Watch yourself," she said through the open window.

He winked and saluted. "Yes, ma'am."

Inside the house he grabbed his guitar, went to the porch, and sat on the swing. Mabel and Cora couldn't be right about everything. Could they? He had to give the relationship at least one more try.

Ray strummed a few cords and let the music sooth his soul. He closed his eyes and launched into the latest love song he'd written. The lyrics about "forever love" didn't jibe with his present situation—especially the lines on friendship and trust. So many questions swirled in his mind. Was Bailey his friend? Shouldn't a romance be built on a strong friendship? Most important—could he ever really trust her again?

So many questions and no answers.

He heard a foot on the step and the snuffle of a dog. He opened his eyes. Faith was standing on the porch holding Sparkles. Meeting her eyes, his heart paused, and he silenced the instrument with his hand.

ॐ

"Please, don't stop playing." Faith settled into a lawn chair beside him. "That was beautiful, Ray."

"You think?" He looked thoughtful. "How long have you been listening?"

"Long enough to. . ." *hear about love, trust, and friendship.* Feeling like an eavesdropper, she held that back. "Long enough to know it's a beautiful song. Did you write it?"

Ray settled back and stretched his long legs out in front of him. "Yes, I did." Smiling, he peered at her intently, and a rush of heat warmed her cheeks.

"What?" she asked. A nervous laugh escaped her lips. "What is it?"

"I don't know." He set down the guitar and gave her another lingering look that set her pulse to racing.

Why this reaction?

"The lyrics are odd," he said. "They seemed to have come out of nowhere."

"Out of nowhere?" Faith swallowed past the sudden dryness in her throat. "I—I think I know what happened."

Ray tilted his head. "Do you?"

"Maybe when you met with Bailey the other night, all those old feelings came back and with them, the lyrics."

Eyes narrowed, Ray appeared to be considering her theory. Then he looked at her and shook his head. "No, that's not it. The lyrics came before I saw Bailey. A few nights ago, when I was trying to sleep." He put his guitar in its case. "I've been thinking a lot about friendship and trust."

"And?" she asked, holding her breath.

He didn't answer, just looked out across the yard.

"Ray?"

He looked back at her. "I'm not sure, but I do know that things aren't what I thought they would be."

His words might have been puzzling to anyone else, but not to her. She knew exactly what he meant.

He sat up, and the pensive Ray was gone, replaced by what she could only describe as "cop Ray." She was disappointed and relieved at the same time.

"So, I've got official permission to look into the break-ins in the area. Can't make an official report yet, though." He glanced at her. "Hard to explain, but if it's official, it goes into an FBI database, and we don't like to do that until what's happening is determined to be a real crime." He smiled. "Not that we don't believe something is really happening."

"That's fine." Her mind snapped back to the business at hand. "Who breaks in just to steal food? I own expensive photography equipment, and it's still there. It's got to be that little girl."

Ray got to his feet. "I'll put my guitar inside. Then let's go over to your place, and I'll check it out."

She waited for him and remembered the other news she had.

"I got a call about Sparkles," she said as they strolled across the lawn toward her house. "A man called in answer to my ad."

Ray stopped and looked down at her. "You don't sound happy."

"I'm not on several levels. I guess I have gotten attached, but I always knew she belonged to someone else, so I didn't let my heart go. My bigger issue is that I don't know how she got hurt. I can't let her go until I determine it wasn't her owner. His name is Peter. He's coming by tomorrow night."

"That makes sense." They stepped through her front door. Sparkles greeted them with little yips, then grabbed a toy and began running in circles.

"I call that her 'crazy dog' response," Faith said. "She does it when she's happy."

Ray smiled, then sniffed. "Smells good in here."

"I had a homemaker attack. While you're here you can try my new double-chocolate chocolate chip cookie recipe."

"Cookies, hmm. You know the way to a man's heart," he joked.

Faith blinked and walked to the counter. Why did those words make her think, *I only wish*? "You want coffee?" Faith scooped coffee grounds into the filter.

"Sure. Hey, you mind if I look at these?"

Faith glanced over her shoulder and saw him pointing at a photo album. "Not at all."

After she finished the coffee, she stood beside him at the table, watching him flip through the pictures, one by one. Mabel, Cora, landscapes of the area. Sparkles. The last two were of him sitting on the porch with his guitar. Faith had caught him with a look of what? Melancholy?

"I'm sorry. I'm not spying on you."

"I know you're not. I've seen you with your camera. I knew what you were doing." Ray's muscled forearm brushed hers, and she felt her skin heat.

"Something wrong?" he asked.

"No, of course not." She turned and pulled mugs from the cupboard, then glanced at him. He had that cop expression, like he didn't seem satisfied with her answer. "I—I guess I'm just nervous about the break-in stuff."

"I understand." Ray cleared his throat. "Hey, how'd your date go, by the way?"

"My date?" Faith sat in a chair at the kitchen table, lest the strength in her legs fail her. "That question came out of nowhere."

Ray shrugged. "Yeah, I guess so. But you haven't answered me."

She could give him the truth—that she'd spent half the evening with George comparing him to Ray. Why, she didn't know. Instead she shrugged. "Actually, George is a great guy. He's funny, too." She laughed to prove her point.

Ray pursed his lips and nodded. "Funny? How so?"

Faith's back stiffened. It was just like Ray to put her on the spot, dig for more. "You're a real cop today, you know that?"

He laughed. "We're friends, we can vent to one another. I pretty much tell you everything that goes on in my life. Speaking of which"—Ray glanced at his watch—"I'm going to see Bailey tonight. Wish me luck."

Luck? He'd need more than luck to get himself straightened out about Bailey. "I'll pray for you—that God will show you the truth."

"Whoa, now you sound like the two women I live with." He jutted his thumb in the direction of the sisters' house, and Faith couldn't help but laugh. "That was a slip of the tongue," Ray said. "I'll take the prayer any day before I wait for dumb luck."

The gurgle of the coffeepot sent relief through her. Faith jumped up and went to the counter, fighting the odd feelings bubbling up inside her. She wanted to laugh, to cry, to slip her arms around Ray and rest her head against his chest. What was happening to her?

"You never did tell me about your date," Ray said from his seat at the table.

That was Ray—he wouldn't let it go. He cared about her as a friend and was only looking out for her well-being. She should appreciate his brotherly concern, so why was she irritated?

Faith brought his cup to the table along with three cookies. He thanked her, and she took her seat beside him. Sparkles, worn out from her play, settled on the floor at their feet.

"Nothing for you to eat?" Ray's dark brows scrunched together.

How could she explain she was too confused to eat, and she didn't know why? "Not right now." She smiled. "So, about my date. . .George has a dry sense of humor, and you know how I like that." Not dry enough to make her forget Ray.

Ray swallowed a large bite of cookie and moaned his contentment. "Delicious." He took a sip of coffee. "Actually, I didn't know you liked that kind of humor. Is that like slapstick or something?"

She suddenly felt defensive. "I can't explain it, and it's beside the point. The thing is, I'm going to give it another chance. We're going out tomorrow night."

"Aha, so you are reluctant. 'Another chance' means you weren't gung ho."

Faith crossed her arms over her midsection. "You're giving Bailey 'another chance.' Are you not gung ho?"

Ray nodded slowly. "Point well taken." He set down his cup and looked her in the eye in that unnerving way of his, like she was transparent under his dark gaze. "I'm not gung ho, Faith. What she did to me. . ." He tapped his fingers on the table. "You said something a couple minutes ago that sort of resonated in me."

"What?"

"It was about Sparkles. You said, 'I guess I have gotten attached, but I always knew she belonged to someone else, so I didn't let my heart go.' I wonder if in a weird way that's how I feel about Bailey. I can't let my heart go anymore because she belonged to someone else."

Hurt shone in his eyes, and her heart squeezed in her chest. "I'm sorry, Ray. You guys had a history together. I shouldn't have compared you with my situation with George." What had gotten into her? Every time she heard him speak Bailey's name, a mean streak surfaced.

"Not a problem." Ray finished the cookie and winked. "Thanks. Delicious." He stood, suddenly all business. "Now, let me get to making a list of your missing property."

She'd really done it this time—she and her big mouth.

fourteen

Ray leaned back on the soft cushions of the blue couch in Mabel and Cora's living room, once again feeling like he'd taken a trip back in time. The only thing that had changed since he was a kid was a fresh coat of yellow paint in the homey room. He shuffled through pages of music in a notebook, asking the Lord to lead him in picking out songs for the following Sunday. Pastor Gary had asked him to lead the worship again on Sunday morning. Ray had chosen an initial upbeat song in the key of *D*. He needed a couple more, then he would modulate to *G*. Both easy keys for the instrumentalists to play, especially the novice guitar player who was new on the worship team.

He picked up his guitar, and as he softly strummed, Mabel and Cora came and stood in the doorway wearing their "going out" dresses.

"I suppose you're seeing *her* tonight?" Mabel said.

"Yes, I am." Ray wondered how they knew.

"We figured." Cora frowned. "It was inevitable."

"You both look gorgeous. Going somewhere special?"

"To the chiropractor and then to do some research on the Victorian." Mabel had her leather briefcase in hand and set it on the floor next to her feet.

"Chiropractor, eh?" Ray winked at Cora.

She blushed, but Mabel was frowning.

He put his guitar down. "What's wrong? I recognize that look. What did I do? Besides make a date with Bailey."

Mabel snorted, then put her hands on her hips. "Young man, you need to tell us when you eat things from the refrigerator. You're not a teenager anymore. You should know better, eating in the middle of the night. It's not good for your digestion. You'll get an ulcer."

"Or that acid reflux." Cora shook her head. "Destroys your esophagus. Then eats the throat away."

"Can't have that," Mabel said. "If you're that hungry, we'll make a bigger dinner."

Her words reminded him of the many lectures he'd gotten from her over the years. But this time he hadn't earned it. "I didn't eat anything from the refrigerator. And if you make dinner any bigger, I'll be big as a house in a month."

Mabel's frown grew. "You didn't eat any midnight snacks? You used to."

"Yes, I know. I *used* to do a lot of things I don't do now. No. The only things I eat are what Cora makes and sets on the table."

The sisters exchanged glances, then looked at him again. "Someone's been in the refrigerator."

Ray sat up, and a page of music drifted to the floor. "You mean *that* much stuff is missing? You can't be mistaken?"

"Mistaken?" Cora clucked her tongue again.

"Don't be a smarty-pants," Mabel said. "Seems we'd know what's in our own refrigerator, wouldn't we?"

Ray stood. "Believe me, I'm not being a smarty-pants. Please show me."

On the way to the kitchen he explained his suspicions about the kid in the neighborhood, telling them that Faith was missing food, too.

"Oh my," Cora said. "Poor dear. Maybe we should leave the door unlocked so she can come in and eat."

As he scanned the room, Ray shook his head. "Miss Cora, no. I know your intentions are good, but I don't think you understand what kids are capable of."

"Maybe we'll leave food on the back porch then," Mabel said. "We can't have a child going hungry."

"No, please don't. That could encourage more bad behavior. I'm investigating the break-ins. I'll make a report about this. I have to catch her."

The sisters glared at him as if one entity.

"I'm a cop." He shrugged, feeling guilty. "I have rules to follow. And the world isn't nirvana."

"Nirvana? Well, I should say not." Mabel swatted at him. "Don't you go talking about that kind of thing in this house, young man."

"It's only a figure of speech," he mumbled.

"Nirvana, indeed," Cora muttered. "But don't you worry none. We're going to pray about this poor child. God is merciful. He isn't tied down by petty police rules."

"Preach it, sister," Mabel said and pointed at Ray's notebook. "Now you go back to your worship."

"And you promise me you'll keep your doors locked."

His concern seemed to get through to them. They didn't argue.

Ray had to force his mind back to the music as he listened to them drive away. He found a likely song and began to play, singing again, imagining the other instruments playing along. When his cell phone vibrated on his belt, he debated whether or not to pick it up. He hated the interruption, but it might be work. Or Philip. Or the pastor. Or. . .Faith.

He pulled the phone from its holder, looked at the screen, then smiled and hit the TALK button. "Faith, what's up?"

"Ray, I'm sorry to disturb you, but Sparkles is missing." Her voice was higher pitched than normal.

"Missing from your house? Your yard?"

"My house. Totally gone."

"Signs of a break-in?"

She paused and inhaled. "I don't know."

"I'll be right over." He set aside his guitar and music and left the house, locking the door behind him. The conversation with Mabel and Cora made him realize that whether he was pursuing justice with a badge or leading worship at church, he needed to continually pray, and he did as he jogged the distance to Faith's front door where she waited, hand to her heart.

"Ray, I'm not sure what to do. Sparkles isn't mine. Really,

I shouldn't have brought her home without her owner's permission, but as you know, I had my suspicions about the injury. I told you the owner was supposed to come by this evening, but I called him and told him not to. I didn't tell him why."

"I'll help you look for her." He impulsively put his arm around her shoulders. She leaned into him for a moment, then stiffened. He let go, surprised that touching her still felt so good, like when they were teens, and he was disappointed she didn't seem to want the contact. "Show me where she was last," he said.

"Okay, okay. . ." Faith led him into the living room and pointed to the sofa. "Sparkles was right there. Right there, curled up on that corner pillow." She looked up at him with worried eyes. "I went to the backyard to put seed in the bird feeder, so I wouldn't have heard anything."

"Did you lock your front door?"

She sighed. "I left the screen door open, and no, I didn't lock it. Anyway, I figured Sparkles would bark."

Ray remained outwardly calm, but the thought that someone had been brazen enough to enter her home while she was there turned his stomach.

"I know it was stupid." She read his expression, although not entirely correctly. "With that child wandering around—"

"Well, I wouldn't go as far as to say stupid, but we all do need to be cautious. Kids, even younger children, are capable of crime. And I don't care where someone lives, the doors need to be locked, even the screen doors. And—"

"And what?"

"For now, I'd recommend you not use the screen door for a breeze. Open windows. Screen doors are too easy to get through."

"Do you think that little girl was in my house again? And maybe took the dog?"

He shrugged. "Could be. You've looked all over the house, right?"

She nodded. "Yes, but you're welcome to do so again if you wish."

He did wish and followed her. He remembered the layout from when her grandmother lived here, but things had changed. A new coat of paint throughout and the wood floors had been refinished. Everything was spotless, like a model home.

"Do you have belongings?" he murmured as he checked the second bathroom. "I think maybe you're only pretending to live here. It's...perfect."

She socked him lightly in the shoulder with her fist. "I told you, I'm a neat freak."

"Ow!" He howled. "Brutality. And here I am being nice to you."

"Arrest me," she said and laughed.

After a check of everything, Ray found nothing of interest. They went back to the living room. "Well, let's not waste time. Let's go look around the neighborhood. Remember, I first found her in the hedges."

Faith pulled on her sweater. "True."

He paused. "So, why did you ask the guy to come by here and not your clinic?"

"Besides the fact that I wasn't scheduled to work today, I wanted to gauge the dog's reaction to him in a home-type setting. I just didn't like the fact that she might have been kicked around, and she didn't have tags. I had also planned to have a friend from a rescue organization here with me."

He groaned and motioned for her to follow him outside.

"What?" she demanded. "What are you griping about?"

He shook his head. "I've been a cop too long. I never give anyone information about where I live. I don't care what the reason."

"Hmm. I hadn't thought about that. I suppose I shouldn't have."

"No matter. I'm right next door."

She smiled. "That you are."

They began their search in the bushes where he'd found the dog, then headed down the street. After several minutes, she appeared so dejected he almost slung his arm around her shoulders, like old times, but Faith was all grown up now and obviously didn't want that kind of attention from him. He stuffed his hands in his jean pockets as they walked down the road in the other direction. Soon it was obvious Sparkles wasn't anywhere to be found.

"Only one last place to look," Ray said as they walked back toward home.

"The old Victorian," Faith said. "Remember we used to say it was haunted? And remember the man who used to live there? I wonder if he's still alive."

"His sister is living down the street with her husband." Ray picked up his pace. "But I don't know about him. I do remember they were on the 'outs' because he inherited the house and she didn't. Mabel and Cora would probably know more." He grinned down at her. "Yeah, I remember nights sitting outside with you, and we'd make up stories about what went on in that house."

They crossed the yard, crowded with overgrown bushes and evergreens.

"Do you think Sparkles or the kid are inside?" Faith peered in a window. "Looks cluttered in there."

"They bought it with a lot of the furniture," Ray said. "And I can't imagine the kid being in there with all the activity lately, with the closing and walk-through. Mabel and Cora have been over here every day as well. There'd be no way the kid could hide." Ray poked through the shrubbery, but found no sign of the dog. "But if that kid has Sparkles, it'll make her easier to find. And I think I have enough now to make this an official investigation." He told her about food missing from Mabel and Cora's house. "I'll talk to my supervisor tomorrow."

They headed back across the street to her house.

"I'll call the SPCA and put them on notice to watch for Sparkles. I do pro bono work for them; they'll help me out."

Faith sighed. "Thanks for being here, Ray."

"Hey, you don't have to thank me. I want to be here for you—and find Sparkles, too."

Faith smiled. "You never change, do you?"

"How do you mean that? Mabel and Cora say the same thing." Ray gave her a sidelong glance.

"Just that we haven't seen each other in years and yet here you are, helping me, just like you used to. Not only that, you seem to bring out the best in me." Faith's face colored.

Ray stopped midstep, turned to her, and took her hands in his. "I think that's the nicest thing anybody's ever said to me. . .that I bring out the best in them." For sure Bailey never spoke anything close to that, and he felt the sting to his core. "You know, you bring out the best in me, too, Faith."

"Do I? How so?"

"You, accepting me at face value. You're probably the only person on the planet who knows me inside out."

She squeezed his hands and smiled. "Ditto. It's nice to be with someone who knows me so well. Someone who doesn't mind my humanness." Faith glanced at her watch. "I've got to get ready for my date with George tonight."

"Hmm." Ray nodded. "You think anything will come of it?" She frowned, and he went on to clarify. "I didn't mean that you had to have marriage in mind to go on a date. But wondered if you thought it might be a possibility."

"I don't know. He's a great guy. This'll be the second time we've gone out. Really, I'm not good at the getting-to-know-you phase of dating. I like the familiar." Faith clamped her teeth on her lower lip as though to stop her flow of words.

"Hey, I'm familiar." Ray laughed, but had to wonder why he felt unsettled about her going on a date and even more so about George being a permanent part of her life. Perhaps he was falling back into the protective role, maybe a big-brother thing. "I'm going out with Bailey tonight."

She eyed him with an unreadable expression. "Aha, so you like the familiar, too."

"Possibly," he said. *Or maybe I'm just a sore loser who has to win back what he lost?* The thought was disturbing. It meant seeing Bailey was more about ego than love. "Okay, I'd better get a move on."

Faith went inside her house, and Ray jogged across the lawn, hoping to outrun the fire burning in his chest. He reached the house, then heard the slam of a car door and turned.

A blond man was climbing from a blue Ford pickup truck. Was that Faith's date?

fifteen

"I'm sorry," Faith repeated to Peter, the man who had called about Sparkles, who stood at her door. His bulk blocked the light coming into the house. "I called and left you a message. Told you not to come tonight. The dog isn't here." She glanced at her watch and tried to quell her irritation. The search for Sparkles had taken longer than she planned. George would arrive in less than an hour, and she wasn't quite ready to go.

"Where is it?" he asked.

It? Didn't he know the sex of the dog? "Not here at the moment. Did you bring proof that the dog is yours?"

His face grew red. "I want my dog. I could sue you."

Being sued was always in the back of her mind as a vet and owner of a clinic. The fact that he prodded that fear pushed her irritation to anger. "Yes, you could. And then I would point out that the dog had no collar and no tags. That's irresponsible. As far as we could tell, *it* was a stray. I cared for the dog myself rather than take her to the pound. If you want to pursue this legally—"

"Are you threatening me?" He took a step toward her.

Faith's irritation grew, but she also felt a bit vulnerable. The man was big. "I'm reminding you that I treated a dog for which I had no guarantee of ever being paid." She had a guarded feeling about the man standing in front of her. "What did you say the dog's name was?"

"I don't have to pay for anything I didn't authorize," he said, his stance challenging her.

Faith threw her shoulders back and slipped around his large frame, letting her door fall shut behind her, and stood at the top of the porch stairs. "I'm expecting company. I'll call you and keep you updated. Next time bring proof the dog is yours. What did you say your last name is?" She tried to make eye contact, but his heavy lids hooded his eyes.

"Yeah, yeah, my last name's Davis. What about it?"

Faith looked across the yard, and her heart jolted. "Ray, hi there!" He stood on the sisters' porch, muscled arms crossed. "Oh, there's my neighbor." She pointed. "He's a cop. He's as interested as I am in getting the dog back to its rightful owner."

Peter narrowed his eyes.

"I'll call you soon, and we can arrange another time for you to pick up the dog."

"Right. Good." He gave her one last scathing look and hurried down the sidewalk to his truck, jumped inside, and took off.

Ray walked across the lawn, and his gaze followed the truck. He reached her and frowned. "Was that George? Did he leave you stranded?"

Did she look desperate? "No, that *wasn't* George. No date of mine would leave me like that." Faith tamped down her irritation now that Peter was gone, narrowed her eyes, and pulled in a breath. "That man was a bully, and I don't date bullies."

"Takes one to know one, I guess." Ray winked, glanced at her again, then grew serious.

Warmed by his affectionate humor, she smiled. Still the tease, Ray was adorable. "That was Peter, the dog owner. Well, he says he's Sparkles's owner, but didn't refer to her by sex or name. I guess the dog could have belonged to one of his kids or something, and he's not that engaged with them. But I got a bad feeling from him."

Ray's brows were furrowed. "I should have gotten his license plate number."

She shrugged. "How would you know he was weird? I'm supposed to call him and tell him when it's convenient to come see the dog again."

"If you do that, tell me. I'd like to be here."

"Will do." She glanced at her watch. "I've got to get ready. George will be here in just a few minutes. Fortunately it's not formal."

"Have a good time," Ray mumbled. "My date isn't for another few hours." He started across the lawn.

"You have a good time with Bailey as well," Faith called out, but her heart wasn't in her fond farewell.

৯

I'm not spying, Ray decided as he settled on the front porch with his guitar. If he happened to catch a glimpse of Faith's date, so be it. What was Faith's type? When they were teenagers, she never kept posters of movie stars on her walls. She never had a steady boyfriend back then that he knew of. Always focused on her goals, she carried a day planner even as a teen. He wondered if she'd had a serious relationship as an adult. Or if she'd ever been engaged.

Ray picked at the guitar strings with no particular song in mind. Tonight he'd find out if there was anything left to salvage of his relationship with Bailey. He ought to be looking forward to their time together—but he felt neither joy nor sadness. Odd after the anticipation he'd felt when he knew he was returning to Bothell, knowing she was available again. He searched his heart, frustrated that he couldn't put a name to his emotions.

The rev of a car engine grabbed his attention. Ray leaned forward in his chair, unsure if the foliage around the porch hid him from view. A man got out of a red Chevy Malibu, and Faith stepped out onto her porch to greet him. She was smiling.

"George," Ray muttered. He was tall and had to lean down to kiss Faith on the cheek. A flare of some strong emotion went off in Ray's chest. For sure, he wasn't angry. Odd that he was so emotionally confused tonight. He shook his head. "What's up with me?" He wasn't Faith's bodyguard, he was her friend. Still, wasn't the guy acting too familiar with her? It was only a second date.

Ray settled back in his chair. Who was he to judge? He'd kissed Bailey on the lips on their second date. He let that thought rattle around in his head for a while, stood, and took another look across the yard. Yeah, but that was Bailey. Faith was different. She was always conservative. Chaste.

Faith looked up, and Ray knew he was busted. He made a show of waving a big hello.

She smiled, that little smile he loved so much, then nodded a hello. Her date held open the car door for her, and Faith got in without giving Ray another look.

Ray drew a deep breath and went inside the house. He was going to see Bailey tonight—that was probably a good thing. He had to get his mind off Faith. It was none of his business whom she dated.

sixteen

Bailey patted her soft blond hair and looked him in the eye. "Great place," she said again, then glanced around the dining room in Canyons.

They were seated one table away from where he and Faith had been sitting. He'd enjoyed that meal, which was probably why he wanted to return. The only spoiler had been their conversation about Bailey. Maybe it was a mistake to take Bailey here. He wanted to remember Faith sitting across from him.

"I've been thinking about us," Ray said, then speared a piece of steak. He suddenly became aware that his plate was almost clean, but Bailey had hardly touched her food.

"Me, too," Bailey said hopefully. "I know it's a big deal to ask you to forgive me. I'm not stupid. I can't really say I'd forgive you if you'd done the same to me." She swiped a tear from the corner of her eye.

Ray set down his fork. "I appreciate your honesty, but it's not about forgiveness." He paused. "Well, that's not exactly true. I am struggling with forgiveness, but it goes deeper. I don't know if what we had is still there, Bailey." She looked on the verge of tears, and he hesitated to continue, but this meeting was about getting it all out on the table. "My feelings for you. . .over the past year, my feelings have run the gamut. It's not a matter of recovering what's lost. It's starting over. I can try—"

"We have to try." Her voiced was high-pitched and panicked. "You don't think we deserve one more chance? Think about how wonderful it was!"

He tried to call back to memory the good times. There had definitely been a strong physical attraction, and they'd had laughs together. But. . .his gaze snapped to hers. "Do you think I've got a good sense of humor?"

Bailey blinked. "Talk about out of left field." Her brows arched. "Is that the criteria? If I think you're funny"—her tone got lighter—"we can date again?" She laughed.

Ray shrugged. In all fairness to Bailey, the question was out of line. He knew why he'd asked—Faith said George was funny, and he wanted to know how his sense of humor compared.

"Of course you're funny," Bailey said. "I think you're wonderful." She reached across the table for his hand.

He gripped hers for a moment, and when the waiter arrived, he let go. He ordered regular coffee and Bailey ordered decaf, then Ray settled back in his chair and leveled a gaze at Bailey. "Trust is key in a relationship. Before anything can be repaired, you and I need to discuss what happened. I want to know why your relationship with Dwight ended."

She colored and glanced at the table. "I guess you could say he ended it."

"He ended it?" Ray's muscles tensed.

"Well, yes. He—he just didn't think we were working out."

Ray unclenched his tight fists. "So is that the only reason you're here? It didn't work out with Dwight?"

Bailey's eyes flashed. "I think it should count for something that *I* didn't end the relationship with him."

"Like you did with me?"

Tears pooled in her eyes. "I can't win here, can I?"

"It's not a matter of winning or losing. I don't know if this hurdle's too big to jump."

She swallowed. "Can you try?"

Their coffee arrived before he could answer, which gave him time to think. For so many months all he'd wanted was to win Bailey back. Now, faced with the reality, he couldn't commit.

He met Bailey's teary gaze. "I can tell you I'll try. I can't give you any guarantees. But you need to give me time. Don't rush me."

Her lips firmed. "I'll prove myself to you. You won't be sorry."

He wasn't so sure.

❧

"You seem a million miles away, Faith." George walked her from the burger joint out to his car with his hand at the small of her back. "Things okay at the clinic?"

"Things are good. Debbie is back full-time now." She was determined to make the best of their date. Get Ray and Bailey off her mind. But the truth was, she didn't want to date George. She didn't see him that way.

"I thought we'd go bowling." George opened the car door for her. "You mentioned you liked bowling."

"Bowling, right." Faith tried to smile. George was trying hard to please. He remembered what she said she liked.

As they rode toward the bowling alley, she looked over at him. George's bushy hair was graying at the temples, which gave him an air of distinction. He wasn't playing at dating. From the first time they'd met when he brought in his dog for shots, she saw the admiration in his eyes. What made her think they could just hang out and be friends? It was now or never.

"George, in all fairness, I've got something I must tell you."

"Uh-oh, I don't like that tone." There was humor in his voice, but he was frowning. He pulled his car into a parking spot in front of the bowling alley and cut the engine. "All right, shoot."

"These, um, dates. . .I'm not ready for a real relationship. I've had a great time with you, but I don't want to give the wrong impression. I see us as friends. If you want more than that—"

"I do," he stated flatly. "I appreciate your honesty, but I don't see you as a female buddy."

"I'm sorry." Faith scanned his face and shrugged. Tonight would only be their second date, but she should've made herself clear from the start. "It's nothing personal. Just that

I've got to focus on my career."

"And you can't do that and have a boyfriend?" George looked at her thoughtfully. "Are you sure you're not commitment phobic?"

"No!" Her shoulders tensed. "At least I don't think so."

"But you're not sure, are you?" He studied her face. "I felt your walls up ever since I met you. I wasn't sure what was wrong, but they were still up during our first date. I thought it was me, but you accepted my second invitation."

"It's not you," she said. "Really."

He patted her arm. "When was the last time you had a boyfriend?"

"A real boyfriend?" She hesitated to say it aloud, glanced at George, and decided she could trust him. "That's easy. It was back in the Navy." But she had never really loved the guy.

"I see." He stared at her for a moment more, then pointed to the building. "You ready?"

"If you'd rather turn around and take me home, that's fine."

"Nope. I can handle this." George smiled and exited the vehicle, came around, and opened the door for her. "This may be God's timing. There's a good chance I'll be transferred to San Diego soon."

A rush of relief came over her and eased a bit of her guilt. "San Diego—that's a beautiful city."

They got their shoes and balls and began to bowl. When they were done, they got colas at the snack bar. George was an exceptionally nice guy; funny, too. Faith found herself wishing she could love him. "I'm pretty sure you won't be on the market for long, George."

He laughed. "That's what my sister says. She's been trying to hook me up with 'the perfect woman for me' for months now. Maybe I should take her up on that. Sometimes our friends and family know us better than we know ourselves."

Faith's thoughts traveled to Cora and Mabel and their matchmaking efforts. "I wonder. . ." She clamped her mouth shut. She'd just told George she was career-minded and had no interest in a romantic relationship.

"What is it?" George tilted his head. "Is there someone? Was that the guy next door?"

Faith felt the color drain from her face. She stared at him, mute.

"I didn't mean to upset you." George took a sip from his can of cola. "But you should've seen your face."

"How did you know about the guy next door?"

"He was watching us as we pulled away."

Faith smiled. Ray had been watching. "That's the guy my friends are trying to set me up with. Yes. But we're only friends. He doesn't think of me that way."

"But you think of him that way, right? You should see your face now, too." George was being a good sport, but she found herself getting more agitated by the second.

"No!" Faith shook her head. "As a matter of fact, he's trying to reconcile with his ex-fiancée."

"I'm sorry." George looked genuinely empathic. "But if it's meant to be—"

"No, no it isn't meant to be." She paused. "What did you mean about my face?"

"What?" George looked baffled, then smiled. "Oh, your face lit up when we started talking about him. What's his name?"

"Ray," she whispered. Her heart flipped. She was in love with Ray.

seventeen

After double-locking her front door, Faith strolled toward the sisters' house, the morning sun warming her head. Would she be able to look Ray eye to eye? Mabel and Cora stood beside the Thunderbird with him like two bodyguards. Before she got within ten feet of them, Mabel pointed at the passenger side door. "Faith, honey, you get in front. Cora and me, we'll sit back here. Ray will do the driving."

"O-kay."

Mabel and Cora sat primly in the backseat, holding almost identical purses in their laps. They were clearly in charge, and today she had no objection to their matchmaking efforts, even though she believed they were wasted. She didn't have the courage to act on what she felt to her core—the revelation had hit hard. Smack dab in the middle of her date with George she knew she was in love with Ray Reed. Perhaps she'd always been in love with him.

Ray glanced at her, and they exchanged a smile, but she couldn't hold his glance. He looked great in a suit. What would Ray think if he could see into her dark heart? He innocently thought of them as friends. He'd trusted her with his deepest secrets—and she'd stayed up half the night praying he wouldn't reconcile with Bailey. Some friend. She'd betrayed his trust. Not that God would honor her selfish prayer.

"So, no sign of Sparkles, eh?" Cora wagged her head.

"None." Faith's heart sank a notch. "I've done all I can."

"I'm sure you have," Cora said.

"Don't you worry none." Mabel nudged her shoulder. "We're prayin'. We have a feeling about this. We think that little puppy is fine. Maybe even with that hungry child."

"We thought the same thing," Faith said. "But if she is, I

wish the girl hadn't come into my house to get her."

"Judith down the street had her bananas taken right out of her car while she was unloading her groceries." Mabel groaned.

Ray's head snapped up. "Why didn't she report it to the police?"

"Because we told her we had a good idea who was doing it. Poor little tyke."

"You find out anything more about her, Ray?" Cora asked. "I worry she's an orphan and she's hungry."

Mabel nodded. "We need to catch her and feed her."

"Like she's a rabbit?" Ray laughed.

Mabel huffed. "Like we did you, smarty-pants."

"You didn't have to catch me. And no, I didn't find out anything else."

"Well, get busy with that," Cora demanded. "Now, you best get us to church. You've got worship to play for."

"Yes, ma'am." Ray smiled, and Faith couldn't help admiring his handsome profile.

"Faith, honey?" Mabel nudged her out of her daydream.

"Yes?" Faith turned to see Mabel's knowing look and prayed Mabel wouldn't give away her secret.

"Would you do me and Cora a big favor?"

"Yes, sure, anything."

"When we start work on the house, we want you to take pictures."

"Yes," Cora said. "Like a diary of how it changes."

Faith smiled. "Absolutely. I'd love to."

Ray shot Faith a covert glance. "Did you talk to Peter again about the dog?"

That was something else that had kept her tossing all night. "No."

"Just remember, don't you ever open the door to him again unless I'm with you, understand?" Ray's face was rigid, his tone adamant.

"I won't." She liked the big, protective side of Ray.

Surprising. She normally hated to be fussed over, especially by a man. She smiled. She loved everything about him. If he ever knew what she was really thinking—

"Ray told us about Peter." Cora sniffed.

"And if Ray's not home, we'll help," Mabel said, slapping her purse. "Nerve of him. You just call us. Cora's got that set of cast iron skillets. Take a man down fast."

Faith giggled, picturing the sisters walloping someone to protect her. Ray reached across the seat and squeezed her hand.

"Huh-uh." Cora laughed. "There you go."

"You two look cute," Mabel said.

Ray released her hand and set his on the steering wheel. "We're not teenagers anymore, Miss Mabel."

"And too bad for that, ain't it?" Mabel moaned.

"What's that supposed to mean?" Ray's brows pulled together.

"Just that some people take detours when what they need is sittin' right there in front of them." Mabel swatted the back of Ray's head, and Faith offered him a sympathetic look.

Of course Ray was frustrated. He must've had a wonderful time with Bailey. She imagined them chatting and laughing. Reminiscing. "How'd it go last night?" Faith blurted and wanted to bite her tongue.

Ray gave her a long look, then indicated with his eyes that they were in mixed company.

"Oh, he had a bad time, yes he did," Mabel uttered, her voice dripping with sympathy.

"Miss Mabel. . ." Ray's jaw clenched.

"Um." Faith sat stiffly. What had she started? "I'm sure he had fun." After opening Pandora's box, she felt obligated to intercede on Ray's behalf.

"Ray's always a gentleman, but he couldn't hide it from us. No sirree." Cora jutted her chin. "It was all those short answers at breakfast. 'Yes, it was fine. Sure, it was fun.' Not the words of a man who had a good time with the woman he wants to spend the rest of his days with."

"Sure ain't," Mabel punctuated.

Ray glanced at Faith. She looked everywhere but at him. She opened the clasp on her handbag and gazed into it. "Anybody have a mint?"

"We know our Ray too well," Cora said, ignoring her question. "God is good."

"Yes, He is." Mabel hummed for a bit. "Faith, darlin', you coming to lunch at our house after church?"

She should decline. The unexpected addition of emotions into her already hectic life would ruin her appetite. And then Ray might see right through to her heart. But on the other hand, her refusal could open a whole new line of questioning she wasn't ready for. "Sure, sounds good."

❧

After church Ray sat at the kitchen table in silence. He mindlessly ate whatever Cora and Mabel set on his plate. His world had been turned upside down during worship. Did anybody notice?

"You played well, son. Even better than last week." Cora's voice was gentle, like she could see the questions churning in his head. "The Lord will show you the way."

His smile was meant to end the conversation. He'd have to make his decisions in the prayer closet—just God and him.

Faith nudged him with her elbow. "Your voice. . ." She set down her fork and sighed. "You're truly anointed, Ray. God gave you an amazing gift."

And therein was the problem. "I don't know. I love playing and singing for the church." Ray settled back in his chair and paused. "But I like being a cop, too. I like protecting Bothell's fine citizens." He half jested to lighten the mood.

"Don't you worry none. It'll all be good. Just like with that little dog. She'll come back. We been prayin'. We got a feeling." Mabel dropped a heaping spoonful of sweet potatoes on Faith's dish. "Well? Faith, honey, how'd your date go last night?"

"Miss Mabel!" Ray stared at her. He appreciated the change of topic, but had to play interception on Faith's behalf.

"Delicious lunch, ladies, I appreciate—"

"It was fine. . . . I mean, yes, we had fun." Faith fumbled with the napkin on her lap.

"Mm-hm." Cora carried the platter of leftover ham to the stove, then returned to the table wearing a bright smile.

"What I thought," Mabel said.

Ray looked at Faith and perceived a storm behind her brown eyes. "Want to go for a walk? We could go to Bothell Landing Park."

"I'd like that. I'll grab my camera." Faith smiled and nodded as the doorbell sounded.

"I'll get that," Cora said.

"Let's go." Ray pulled out Faith's chair for her, ready to make a hasty retreat, then heard Bailey's cheery voice and held back a groan. *Great!* He needed time to think, and Bailey wasn't about to give him the time nor space. Had she always been this pushy? Come to think of it, yes. He had to wonder if Dwight really had done the initial pursuing of Bailey—or had she pursued him?

"It's Bailey!" Cora yelled.

"Bailey," Mabel echoed and looked sadly at Faith and Ray. "No walk in the park. Guess it's time for some Sunday afternoon prayer."

Faith sighed. "I better get home, anyway. I have bills to pay. Don't want to fall behind."

She looked like she could use a friend. "I'm sorry," Ray said just as Bailey flounced into the kitchen behind Cora.

"Ray!" Bailey went to him, wrapped her arms around his neck, and kissed him on the cheek. He pulled back, just slightly. His gaze shot to Faith. She was balling up her napkin, and her lips were narrowed. He wanted to apologize. For what, he didn't exactly know.

"Thanks so much for lunch." Faith stood.

"You don't need to go yet, do you?" Mabel scowled.

Cora stood. "We have pie."

"No, thanks." Faith gave Mabel a hug, then Cora. "Nice

seeing you again, Bailey." She disappeared from the kitchen in a flash.

After a long moment of silence, and several sympathetic moans from the sisters, Cora set a plate at the table next to hers.

"Go on and sit." Mabel pointed at it.

Bailey glanced at the chair next to Ray, but he didn't say anything. He was still pondering why Faith had run off. Bailey finally obeyed and perched on the edge of the chair.

"Would you like some lunch?" Mabel gave Bailey an assessing look, and Ray prayed silently that the sisters wouldn't say anything crazy.

Bailey glanced at the food on the table. "Um, no thanks. I had some sushi and miso soup in town a little while ago."

"Ohh, that's raw fish, ain't it?" Cora stood and murmured, "Pin worms. . ."

Mabel frowned. "Me-soul-soup?"

"Miso. It's a fermented soy product and. . ." Bailey looked at Ray for help.

"Fermented?" Mabel asked. "Isn't that what—"

"It's good soup," Ray said. "I've had it." He patted Bailey's arm. "They don't do Asian food."

"What's wrong with good old country cooking is what I want to know?" Cora said. "Raw fish, indeed. Hmpf."

Ray winked at Bailey, hoping she wouldn't take offense. "I happen to like sushi—"

"I call it bait," Cora interrupted. "We used it to catch catfish when I was growin' up."

Ray accepted that this was a battle he couldn't win. He just smiled.

"Have some iced tea then." Mabel slapped a glass in front of Bailey.

"Does it have sugar?" Bailey bit her lip. It was clear she was trying to be polite. "I'm sorry. I'm just. . .well, I avoid sugar to keep my weight at a good place."

"What kinda tea doesn't have sugar?" Mabel planted her

hands on her hips and looked Bailey up and down. "Besides, you could use a little meat on your bones."

Ray squeezed Bailey's arm and bit back a grin. "It's southern sweet tea. Delicious."

"Well, I can't. . ." Bailey's voice trailed off as the sisters stared at her incredulously. "Um, I'll make an exception. I'm sure it's wonderful." She took a big gulp.

"Why don't we go sit in the living room?" Ray nodded at Bailey.

Mabel and Cora were next to each other, looking like one solid unit.

"We'll be cleaning up," Cora said.

"And praying," Mabel said over her shoulder as she turned to the sink.

"They pray a lot," Bailey whispered when they reached the living room.

"You don't know the half of it." Ray took her arm to lead her to the sofa when Bailey turned to him.

"Can we sit out on the porch instead?" She looked over her shoulder at the kitchen door.

"Sure." He held the door open for her, and they settled into chairs on the porch.

"You can pour that into the bushes, if you'd rather not drink it." Ray pointed at the glass of tea she held in her clenched fist.

"Are you sure?" Her gaze settled nervously on the windows as if she was afraid Mabel and Cora were watching.

"Here, I'll take it." He pried it from her hand and downed it with three gulps.

"Thank you," she said.

"You're welcome. You don't need to worry. Mabel and Cora are sweet, but opinionated and sometimes overbearing. You just gotta go with the flow."

"I guess." Bailey's voice was small.

Ray put the glass on the floor. "Okay, I don't want to be rude, but why are you here? I told you I needed some time to think—"

"I know." She slipped her hand in his. Her smile was shaky, unsure. "It's just that I stayed up all night thinking about you. About us. I couldn't wait another minute to talk to you."

"You could've called. It's not like I wouldn't take your call."

Her eyes teared, and Ray took her other hand in his. "I'm not going to lie to you. I don't know if this relationship can be fixed."

Bailey sniffled. "That's why I knew I had to come over today. We need to talk. I don't want to lose you." She squeezed his fingers. "I made the biggest mistake of my life dating Dwight. I love you, Ray. I've loved you all along. I guess I never learned coping skills. I felt ignored, and I did the next best thing."

Ray leaned forward and hugged her. It hurt to know he was the cause of her tears. "I forgive you, Bailey, but I just don't know."

"Please?" Bailey leaned back and looked into his eyes. "A few more dates. How can that hurt? I believe in my heart we're worth another chance."

What could it hurt? He pondered the question, recalled their good times together. They'd been so in love once. Ray drew a breath and nodded, then heard the slam of a door.

Bailey glanced over his shoulder, and her eyes narrowed. He turned to follow her gaze. Faith was rushing toward the house, crossing the yard in a steady jog.

She stopped at the bottom of the porch steps. "I'm so sorry to interrupt but—"

"That's okay. What's wrong?" Ray offered Bailey an apologetic nod and stood.

Faith's face was set, almost angry. "It's my back porch and the back door."

Ray walked down the stairs. "What?"

"I went in the front door and walked down the hall to the back door. It was open. There's dog food spilled all over the porch. It might be that kid, and it makes me nervous. I don't know if anybody's still in the house. Food is missing again, too."

"I'll go check things out now." Ray turned to see Bailey,

arms crossed tight against her midsection, anger emanating from her eyes.

"I'll be back," he said.

Mad as Bailey looked, Faith's safety took precedence.

"I'll go with you," Faith said.

"No. You and Bailey go inside."

"It's fine," Bailey said. "I have somewhere to go. I'll call you later, Ray." She glanced at Faith. "You're in good hands."

eighteen

"I'll be there, Miss Mabel," Ray said into his cell. He clicked the OFF button and put the phone on his belt.

Philip walked into his cubicle and dropped onto a chair.

Ray eyed his brother. "You look exhausted."

Philip stifled another yawn. "I think single life is catching up with me."

Ray shook his head. "Still the playboy—out all hours. Even on a Sunday night?"

Philip grinned. "At least I'm not tied down."

"Well, I'm not either anymore, but I do get decent sleep." Ray laughed when Philip slumped in his chair and pretended to snore. "Maybe I shouldn't ask, but what are you doing after work?"

Philip sat up. "What? Why? Will there be pretty girls there?"

"Oh brother!" Ray shook his head. "Pretty girls? Yes. Cora and Mabel."

Philip grinned. "Beautiful inside and out. If I could find a woman that good—and that good in the kitchen." He sighed. "That could be the ticket. These women I'm dating. . .doesn't anybody cook anymore?"

"Gotta look in the right places for them." Ray thought he should take a dose of his own advice.

"So what's up?"

"That was Mabel on the phone. She and Cora want me to start measuring at the Victorian, make a supply list. Faith's coming to take pictures. You up for that? I need your input since you'll be helping me anyway."

Philip rubbed his eyes and his stomach, then groaned dramatically. "Can we eat first?"

"I've got one better for you. Cora's bringing over her fried

117

chicken. They want to celebrate in the new place. Good?"

"I'm there." Philip grabbed his car keys off the desk. "And it'll be good to see Faith again. Give me an hour."

❧

Ray walked across the street to the Victorian while dialing Faith's cell number.

"Hello, Ray."

The sound of her cheery voice brought a smile to his face. "Did Mabel and Cora call you and tell you the good news?

"Yep. That's why I'm home. Debbie is working her normal evening shift. I'm coming over in a minute after I finish changing."

"I'm at the Victorian. They gave me a key and one for you, too. If you come over now, we can explore before all that energy arrives in the form of two sisters we both know and love."

She laughed. "You've got that right."

Minutes later Faith arrived, camera hanging around her neck. Ray held the front door open for her, and she brushed past him smelling of perfume and shampoo with just a faint touch of antiseptic, a scent he was beginning to associate with her.

For a moment he thought she was going to hug him, but she didn't hold his gaze. Instead she began to look around the foyer.

"Wow. This is amazing." She wandered from the foyer to the wood-floored hallway. "And the mess is amazing, too."

Old furniture crowded the rooms. It was difficult to distinguish clutter from trash. "Yeah. The owner is in a nursing home apparently, and his family didn't take the time to clean things out. Well, except for some of the nicer antiques. They made sure to take those, and they made a mess while they pawed through stuff. But the sisters bought it as is."

"They'll find some treasures in here, I'm sure." Faith looked cute in her jeans and T-shirt. Nothing fancy, but it suited her. "Look at this molding." She snapped a picture. "And that staircase." She took another.

"And especially note all the work that needs to be done,"

Ray muttered, tugging on a hanging strip of wallpaper.

She aimed her camera at him. "That's what you experts are here for."

He posed, pretending to wipe sweat from his brow.

"Do a muscleman," she said.

He struck a weight-lifter stance.

She laughed, a contagious sound that he couldn't help but join. "We've got our work cut out for us, that's for sure."

Faith snapped another picture, then looked pensive. "Did you check for signs of that kid being in here? Or Sparkles?"

"I did a quick walk-through before you got here, but it's hard to tell if things were left by the owner or by someone in the house."

"What did you find?"

"A banana peel in a trash can and a couple of apple cores."

"Well that wouldn't be from the previous owner, but maybe Cora and Mabel ate here."

He shrugged. "Could be. We'll ask them. The front door was locked. I didn't hear or see anything unusual."

She began clicking more pictures, and he walked into a large room to the left, off which were two sets of french doors.

"If I understand things right, this is going to be a dining area." Ray scanned the room, imagined what it could be, and smiled. "They want to have tables outside on the terrace in warm weather."

More camera clicks behind him. "Got it," Faith whispered.

He gave her a lingering look as she walked past him into the room. She seemed to be blooming before his very eyes. Hair wild, a smile on her face, she was in her element doing what she loved. She looked. . .good. He intentionally glanced away and focused on the fireplace mantel made from bird's-eye maple. "Lots of work here, too."

"This is amazing," Faith said. "I would love to live in a house like this, but you know what my dream house is?" As though the hearth had been ignited, Faith's warmth filled the high-ceilinged room.

"No, tell me. What's your dream house?"

"Hands down, Mabel and Cora's place. It's so. . ." She walked to the right set of french doors and grabbed the handle. "Homey. I feel at home there."

"I thought you loved your grandmother's house."

"I do, but it's not big enough to raise a family in."

Faith's face took on a dreamy glow. "If I had the money, I'd buy Cora and Mabel's house. It would be great for a family—if I ever have a family." She sounded suddenly sad.

Ray patted her back but wanted to yank her into his arms, camera and all. The conversation reminded him of a long ago day she'd been upset about something her father had done and she'd started to cry. Ray had felt so helpless. He hugged her. Now he remembered the feel of her—soft, leaning into him. The slow dawning in her eyes when the hug continued longer than normal. But she'd withdrawn when it was over, and not too long after that, she moved away. No, he couldn't think about her that way.

Ray swiped his hand through his hair and turned away. Why was his mind going that direction? Perhaps insecurity about the decisions he had ahead made him look to the past for good feelings. He took a deep breath and cleared his throat.

"Everyone will be here any minute. And Philip is coming as well."

"Good," she said, disappearing into the room on the opposite side of the hall.

Please, please come soon. Ray felt himself losing the battle. "We'll look through the house when they get here."

"Okay," she called.

Relieved she was out of sight, he tried to focus on the work to be done. What was wrong with him that he couldn't keep his eyes off Faith? He heard the sound of a car engine and voices and breathed a prayer of thanks to the Lord as he walked back to the hallway.

"Yoo-hoo, it's me." Mabel traipsed through the front door,

carrying a picnic basket. Cora followed with two more. "Me and Cora."

Faith appeared. "Smells delicious." She took a basket from Cora. "Which way to the kitchen?"

"Follow me," Mabel said. "It's at the back of the house."

"Let me help." Ray tried to take the other basket from Cora.

"You go out to the car and get the cooler of drinks," Cora ordered.

"You drove *all the way* across the street?" Ray snorted a laugh.

"Yes, Mr. Smarty-Pants. You think we were going to carry all this food?" Mabel said over her shoulder.

"I would have helped you."

Cora and Mabel exchanged glances and tiny grins. "We were giving you time to show Faith around our new place."

Ray shook his head. Matchmakers!

nineteen

Faith glanced around the makeshift table in the kitchen at Ray, Philip, Mabel, and Cora. It was easy. Comfortable. Like those summer meals so long ago when she was young. She hadn't realized until now how much she'd missed this. And just how much she'd missed Ray. Her heart ached thinking she could lose it all again. If he and Bailey got together, that would change everything. Bailey wouldn't want to share Ray. Faith would lose him as a friend. She'd caught enough of her sharp glares the few times they'd been together.

Mabel patted her knee. "Don't you fret now. Take that frown off your face."

"How could anyone frown with all this good food?" Philip said. "Pass more of those mashed potatoes, please." He pointed at the large plastic container.

"Watch it," Ray said. "You won't be able to button your shirt tomorrow."

"Like you?" Philip shot a grin at Ray while he dropped a generous helping on his plate.

"Ray, don't you bother your brother none while he's eating." Mabel blew out a sigh.

Cora nodded. "You always used to do that, you scamp."

Faith smiled. "Really?"

"Yes indeed. Ray would poke and prod Philip until he poked back. Then Ray would play the innocent."

Ray wiggled his eyebrows at Faith, and she giggled.

"Gravy, please," Philip said.

"But he didn't get away with it. No sirree." Mable handed Philip the gravy boat.

"We knew. We always know." Cora hummed under her breath and glanced from Faith to Ray.

"How's work, Philip?" Mabel asked. "You still enjoying your job?"

"Except for the cases I can't solve." He shoveled another spoonful of food into his mouth.

"The gas station robbery," Ray clarified.

Philip nodded. "Attendant is still in a coma. But he's showing signs of coming around."

"I remember reading about that," Faith said. "No witnesses?"

"Not that we can find yet."

"We'll pray for a miracle," Mabel said.

Cora nodded. "God is in control."

Faith sat quietly while everyone finished their meal. She couldn't eat another bite, and surprisingly the sisters let her alone, not nagging her to clean her plate. *This is family,* Faith mused. They talked and shared laughs in that easy way that she'd never known with her real family, even before her mother passed away. She'd always felt like a misfit in her own home.

"Earth to Faith," Ray said, tapping her foot with his under the table.

She blinked. "What?"

Mabel chuckled. "We been talking to you, honey, but you were somewhere else."

"Yes, I guess I was." Not really. She was here, heart and soul.

Cora stood. "Time to tidy things up."

"I'll help you wrap the leftovers." Faith joined Cora.

"You boys start making your list of things that need to be done," Mabel ordered, pointing first at Ray then at Philip.

"From that we'll decide which projects we want done first," Cora said.

"Everything done decently and in order," Faith and Mabel said at the same time.

Everyone laughed, then Ray slapped his brother on the shoulder. "Let's start upstairs."

As she and the sisters repacked the baskets, Faith tried to put her feelings into words. "This is going to sound crazy."

She put lids on the containers. "But I feel like I'm home."

"You are." Mabel tucked foam plates and plasticware into a trash bag. "No hot water here yet. The electricity will be turned on tomorrow. And we ordered us a humongous refrigerator."

"Side-by-side," Cora said with pride in her voice.

"Big enough for three turkeys." Mabel patted Faith's arm. "When will you understand?"

Cora leaned against the counter, smiling.

"What?" Faith looked at the two and shrugged. "What do you mean?"

"Our home is your home. . .and Ray's," Mabel said, and Cora nodded. "But we two best make haste." Mabel eyed her sister.

"Oh yeah." Cora removed her apron. "We've got a prayer meeting at our place with Sister Judith. Huh-uh. We gotta go right now."

Faith helped them load the leftovers in their car and returned with them to the kitchen for more. "Leave the cooler and drinks for Ray and Philip," Mabel ordered.

"Okay, and I guess I'll get going, too. Leave the guys to their work." Faith reached for her camera, but Cora clamped a hand on her arm.

"Can you stay a bit longer? Take more pictures?" Cora asked as Mabel exited the kitchen.

Now what were they up to? Faith shrugged. "I—I guess so."

Cora gave her a warm hug. "Don't bother showing us to the door. We know our way out."

Ray walked into the kitchen with Mabel at his side. Faith's heart sped. She had to get over this—over him—and quick.

"You kids have fun," Mabel said, and the slam of the front door followed shortly.

She stood staring at Ray. If she was supposed to speak, she was at a total loss.

"Did you need me?" Ray clipped the tape measure to his belt and walked toward her.

Faith spread her hands in question. "Need you?"

A frown started at his brows, followed by a slow smile that made her go weak at the knees. "That's what Mabel said."

"Me?" Faith pointed an accusing finger at her shoulder. "I didn't say that."

"Interesting." Ray walked around the table and looked down into her eyes.

"I was helping them clean up. Now I have orders to take pictures. That's all. Just take pictures." Why did she feel guilty? Because she loved Ray's eyes? His muscular arms? "I have no idea why Mabel told you that." Faith tilted her chin defiantly, which brought her eye to eye, nose to nose, and nearly mouth-to-mouth with Ray.

He wrapped his hands around her upper arms, sending warmth through the cotton of her T-shirt. Her breath came faster. With no conscious thought, her hands reached around his neck in a reckless embrace.

Their lips touched, as though she'd been waiting all her life for this moment.

His fingers tightened on her arms. She leaned against him, feeling how strong and solid he was.

"Oops, bad timing."

Faith and Ray jumped apart. Philip stood in the doorway of the kitchen shielding his eyes. "Sorry, folks."

"No, we were just. . ." Faith looked to Ray for rescue, but he seemed glued in place, glancing from her to Philip.

"I'll be upstairs." Philip ducked out of the room in a flash, and she heard his retreating footfalls. Her face heated.

Ray suddenly came to life. "Are you all right?" He rubbed her arm.

She ignored the warmth of his touch. "I'm fine," she snapped, pulling away from him.

"You're mad. Why are you mad?" He frowned.

"If you don't know, I'm not going to explain." She knew her words and tone made her sound irrational, but she felt irrational.

"I have to leave now," she said, afraid if she talked, she'd burst into tears, and she hated weakness.

"Leave? Now?"

"Yes, now."

His eyes glinted. "I'm sorry, Faith. That shouldn't have happened."

His words only made things worse. "I agree." She glared up into his face. "Excuse me, please."

Ray stepped aside. "Fine, but I think we need to talk. I still don't understand why you're angry."

"Later." She slipped out the front door, hurried down the steps, and ran across the street toward her house. "Need to talk, my foot," she whispered.

Faith stepped onto her front porch and skidded to a stop. A tiny, dark form huddled next to her front door. "Sparkles!" She scanned the area before reaching the pup, knelt down, and scooped her up. "You're shivering."

How did she get back here? Faith glanced over her shoulder before unlocking her door. She went inside, set down her camera, and cuddled Sparkles closer to her chest. The little dog frantically licked her chin, then yapped a hello.

Faith grabbed the phone and dialed the sisters' house. She'd have to let them know she'd found Sparkles. . .and tell them to pass the information on to Ray. There was no way she wanted to face Ray Reed again tonight.

twenty

Ray woke early, the bright sun in total opposition to his mood. What had happened? He'd kissed Faith. . .his friend. And liked it. Of course he did. He was a man. Didn't most men like kissing women? And she'd looked and smelled irresistible.

He crawled out of bed and went to the shower. No, kissing Faith hadn't been a mere physical response. He enjoyed it because he liked her. *And* because she looked good. How could he call himself her friend? Sending her mixed signals. Telling her he wanted to reconcile with Bailey one minute, taking her in his arms the next.

After treating himself to a cold shower as punishment, he dressed and peered out the window. The sisters were shopping for wallpaper for the Victorian so he wouldn't have to deal with them. He'd managed to avoid them last night, too, and found the note they'd left explaining that Faith phoned to say she'd found Sparkles on her front lawn. Why hadn't Faith phoned him instead?

Simple, you idiot. She was offended and angry. . .and embarrassed. He'd seen it in her eyes. But would she avoid him forever?

Ray went downstairs, grabbed two sweet rolls from a plastic container on the counter, and hurried out the door. He looked over at Faith's house. She wasn't there. Good. It was best not to see her again until she cooled down. Then he'd try to reason with her. Tell her she had nothing to be embarrassed about.

He went to his car, unable to take his mind off the kiss. Yes, he'd made her uncomfortable and self-conscious. But. . .

She *had* kissed him back. Fastened her hands around his

neck and pulled him closer. He wasn't mistaken about that. He dug his keys from his uniform pocket, but before he could give the matter deeper thought, he saw the kid, this time hanging around in front of the Victorian.

He hustled down the drive. The kid looked over and saw him. Her little mouth opened in a silent *O*, and she broke into a run. Ray gave chase for more than a block, but the kid disappeared between two houses, and Ray couldn't find her.

Even though he wasn't due to work yet, he called dispatch to report in. Before he returned to the Victorian to look around, he stopped at the houses on either side to ask the residents if they were missing things. He got one negative from a woman who worked nights. The other house was owned by a retired couple who said they rarely left home.

Ray suddenly recalled that this was where the sister of the man who had owned the Victorian lived. "One more question," Ray said.

The elderly couple opened the door wider. "Coffee?"

Ray declined but thanked them all the same. "Have you seen a young girl. . .looks to be around ten, eleven? She's got red hair, freckles. Hangs around the neighborhood all day it seems."

"That kid do something?"

"Not that I know of, but I need to find her."

The man studied Ray's face. "My wife was feeding the kid. Dirty little urchin. Had her sleeping in the shed. But I took care of that."

"What do you mean took care of that?"

"I told her to go home," Ernest said. "Edna, she was upset. She treated the kid like a pet. . .when she remembered she was there." His wife went back inside and sat on the sofa, mumbling. "Doctor says it's Alzheimer's," Ernest whispered.

"When did you tell the kid to leave?"

"Last night. She had a dog, too."

"Would you mind showing me the shed?"

Ernest walked Ray around the house and pointed to a

ramshackle wood building. "I never use it. That's why I didn't know the kid was there. But I cleaned it up after the kid left. There was trash here and some dog stuff."

"Why didn't you report this to the police?"

"Police cause me trouble," Ernest grumbled. "Don't like 'em. Sorry."

"I am, too. We're not all bad."

"Could of fooled me." Ernest sounded bitter.

Ray wished he could pursue the conversation but didn't have time. He disliked having his uniform stand between him and people in need—especially those in need of God. Many were often intimidated and even nervous around him.

He pulled out a business card. "I live right down the road at the moment. With Mabel Sanders. If you need anything, call me."

Ernest's face softened for a moment. "Mabel and Cora. Good people." He blinked. "No, I don't think so. I told you, don't have much time for the police." But he took the card anyway.

Ray thanked the man and walked back to the Victorian. What did the kid want? Ray checked all the doors to the Victorian. Everything was locked tight. He walked around the building, noting the overgrown shrubbery. This would all have to be torn down. He noticed some of the plant life was smashed down, probably from the real estate people and the building inspection. He pushed aside the bushes, and behind them was a basement window. He knelt in the dirt and pressed his hand against the window. It was open.

❧

Faith nearly fell over the trash receptacle in her office and kicked it out of her way. It rolled into the hallway, where she left it. "Stupid cleaning people can't put things back," she said to no one in particular as she dropped heavily into her chair. Good thing the clinic wasn't open yet. She was in such a bad mood she wasn't fit for human contact. She yanked some files from her inbox. "What am I looking for?" she mumbled.

"Doc, I'm cleaning cages in the kennel," Lindsey shouted as she walked quickly past her office door.

"Wonderful!" Faith hollered in return as she leaned over her desk to study reports from the lab.

There was a tap on her door, and Gladys peeked into her office. "Dr. Hart?"

"What?" she snapped.

Gladys glanced from her to the trash can in the hall. "Um, I. . ."

Faith stared at her. "What do you need?"

Gladys took a step back. "I just wanted to know if you'd like me to start billing today."

"Yes. It is billing time. It happens the same time every month. And shut my door, please."

Gladys obeyed without saying another word, shutting the door with more force than necessary.

Faith knew she was being obnoxious, but couldn't seem to help herself. Well, that wasn't true. She *could* help herself, but she wasn't trying very hard. She stared at the lab reports, but the words and numbers were like gibberish. Instead, her errant mind insisted on imagining Ray's eyes and lips. She had kissed him—and she'd liked it. She slapped her hand on her desk. If she relived the kiss one more time she might throw more than a trash can across her office.

"Is that the sound of violence I hear? And look, a dented trash can. I wonder who did that." Debbie's voice floated through the door.

It opened, and Faith blew out a long breath. "You of all people should understand. The door is shut for a reason." She glared at her friend.

"I had to make sure you weren't doing anymore damage. We do share the expenses around here." Debbie strolled across the oatmeal-colored Berber, trash receptacle hanging from her fingertips. "Lose this? Looks like someone abused it and put it in the hallway."

"Very funny. Just set it next to my desk."

"Yes, ma'am." Debbie's tone was sarcastic as she placed the receptacle down with exaggerated gentleness. "And I thought I was crabby from lack of sleep with my colicky baby. Your hair is sticking up all over the place. That only happens when you're stressed, and the last time I can remember it being this bad was during final exams in vet school." She crossed her arms. "Everyone is whispering in the office so as not to disturb you, even Lindsey."

Faith felt the bite of guilt. Come to think of it, she was acting a lot like she had in the Navy when she'd been on board ship and sleep deprived. And, like Debbie said, during final exams. *Lord, I am one impatient person.*

"So, what's happened to bring this not-so-charming side of you out?"

"I'm sorry," Faith said. "I called that guy Peter to tell him I found Sparkles again. He's coming by the house this evening."

"So, you found the dog—that's good news. The guy who might be the owner is coming by—and maybe he'll pay the bill. Doubly good news." Debbie frowned. "I don't get it. *That's* why you kicked your trash can into the hall?"

"No." Faith picked up a folder and flipped through it, unseeing. "It's because I have to call Ray. He wants to be there the next time Peter comes by. Says there's something weird about the whole thing. And about Peter." She sighed. "I have to agree. The guy gave me the creeps."

"I don't understand." Debbie's frown deepened, and she leaned against the desk, arms folded. "Ray's a cop. He'll be there to protect you. Why is that bad?"

"That's exactly the problem. *Ray* will be there."

"I admit I haven't had my second cup of coffee, so all my cylinders aren't running yet, but what am I missing? The guy's a creep. Ray is going to keep you safe. Did something happen between you guys?"

"A kiss!" Shame heated her face. "That's what happened." Faith slapped the folder down. Papers slid all over the desk. "And I liked it. Wrong, wrong, wrong."

"What? A kiss? And what's wrong with that?" Debbie laughed, but Faith glared at her, and she sobered. "I'm sorry, but do you know how weird you sound?"

Faith shook her head. "Didn't you hear me? I—kissed—Ray."

"Okay." Debbie's eyes widened. "So why is this so bad?"

Faith glanced at her partner, then counted out on her fingers. "First, he's my best friend. *Was* my best friend. Second, he's still pining for someone else. Third—third. . .I'm so stupid. I think my feelings are more than. . .well, more than friends. . .I'm. . ." She let her voice trail off.

"In love?" Deb asked in a solemn whisper.

Faith ran her finger over the papers that had slipped from the file and let her breath out slowly. "I. . .well. . .maybe." *Yes.*

"I don't think there's any *maybe* about it." Debbie stared at her long and hard. "You're in love. I've been watching you since Ray came into town. You glow. Your eyes sparkle. And you're smiling a whole lot more."

"That can't be right," Faith murmured. She wouldn't admit it aloud. Doing so would make it all too real.

"Ah, love." Debbie sighed. "I remember when Lance and I first met." Her smile lit her face. "We were ice skating at—"

"No, this is different, Deb." Faith closed her eyes to collect her thoughts. "Ray's still got his ex-fiancée on his mind. Worse, I'm afraid I ruined one of the best friendships I've ever had." Tears made her blink. "I intentionally refused a date with Ray when we were teens. I didn't want to ruin our friendship then, and I don't intend to destroy it now."

"Interesting. That's not how you told it back in college. It was your father who put the kibosh on it."

Faith felt the blood drain from her face. Had she been blaming her dad for her fear of failure? "My father was a big, big part of my decision." Not exactly true. If she'd wanted to pursue Ray, she could have. At that point her father might have backed off. Faith had Ray's phone number. She swallowed around the lump in her throat and started again.

"Okay, I didn't want to disappoint my father—"

"And you didn't want to disappoint yourself if things didn't work out," Debbie stated boldly.

"That's beside the point." Faith stood and jammed her hands in the pockets of her jacket. "I want to stay friends with Ray. Friends don't kiss in *that* way."

Debbie rolled her eyes toward the ceiling. "Lord, please help this woman see common sense." She screwed up her face and blew out a breath. "Did you force him to kiss you?"

"No, but I liked it and encouraged it."

"And he didn't push you away? He didn't run screaming in torment because you locked lips?"

Faith shook her head. "Of course not. Don't be facetious. His brother walked into the room."

"Oh, that's rich." Debbie grinned. "I would have loved to be a fly on the wall when those two talked."

Faith blushed again. "Right. How embarrassing is that?"

Debbie straightened and tucked her hair behind her ears. "I think the biggest problem here is that both of you are dumb as rocks."

Faith blinked. "Dumb. . .what?"

"You heard me."

"That's insulting."

"It was meant to be. Now get your act together and quit scaring the staff." Whirling around, Debbie laughed. "I'm leaving before I get hurt by a trash can hurtling through the air." She disappeared out the door, then poked her head around the corner. "By the way, I have a good feeling about things." She withdrew like a turtle.

"A feeling? You sound just like Cora and Mabel!" Faith yelled at the empty doorway. "And right now *all* of you are irritating me."

Debbie's only response was more laughter.

twenty-one

"Ray, here's some joe." Philip pushed a cup of coffee across Ray's desk. "You look like you need it."

"Yeah, thanks." Ray didn't look up from the report he was typing, just snatched the coffee cup and pulled it toward him. He'd hoped his job would take his mind off his personal life, but it wasn't working. Between exhaustion from tossing and turning at night and frustration with so many decisions and so few answers, he could barely think. Not to mention a kid running around the neighborhood breaking into houses and stealing stuff.

"Earth to Ray." Philip waved his hand in front of his face.

Ray glanced up. "Sorry. And thanks for the coffee." He lifted the cup to his mouth.

"Watch out—"

Ray took a big gulp before Philip finished his sentence. The coffee hit his tongue and the roof of his mouth like fire, then burned its way down his throat.

"—it's hot," Philip finished.

Ray set the cup back on the desk and swallowed several times, blinking back tears of pain. "Really hot," he said hoarsely.

"That would be why steam was coming off the top." Philip squinted and waved his hand in front of Ray again. "You all right? Something wrong with your eyes?"

"Don't get smart with me." Ray swallowed again and cleared his throat. "Just because you're older doesn't mean I can't take you down."

"You and what army?" Philip snorted a laugh and flexed his arm. "I've started lifting three days a week. Hired a personal trainer at the gym."

134

"And you're making me feel like a slob." Ray glanced down at his stomach. He was fast developing a paunch.

"Helps relieve the stress of the job," Philip said. "So, what are you working on?"

Ray turned his monitor so Philip could read it. "The break-ins in my neighborhood. This morning I found a basement window open on the sisters' new place. I went inside, but found nothing. I went door-to-door earlier and found out that more locals than I thought have had things stolen. I think I know who the culprit is. This kid who's been hanging around the neighborhood." He explained about the old man's shed and how his wife fed the kid.

"You talking about Ernest and Edna?"

Ray nodded.

"She's the sister to the guy who was living in that monstrosity that Mabel and Cora own now. Bad blood there between them, the brother and sister."

"So I hear," Ray said.

Philip dragged a chair to the side of Ray's desk and stared at the monitor. After a moment, he looked up. "A kid, huh?"

"Yep. She's fast, though. I chased the little bugger through the neighborhood this morning. Couldn't catch her."

Philip laughed. "Maybe you need to cut out Cora's fried chicken and take up jogging."

"You might be joking, but I'm thinking the same thing." Ray sat back in his chair and pointed at the monitor. "Knowing who's doing the breaking in only leads to more questions."

"Doesn't it always?"

Ray nodded. "This kid is tied up with the dog somehow and then tied up with this dude who scared Faith when he came to claim the dog. She left a message for me and said—"

"Left a message?" Philip's brow lifted.

"Yes," Ray said. "She left a message and said the guy is coming by her house in an hour and a half. I told her not to see him again unless I'm there." He shook his head. "I can't believe she gave a stranger her home address to begin with."

"I see." Philip smiled.

"It's not funny," Ray said. "The guy is a creep."

Philip shrugged, still smiling. "Not arguing that point."

He stared at his smirking brother. "Then what?"

"You, being so concerned about your neighbor—Faith."

Ray's frustration boiled to the surface. "I'm a cop," he snapped. "I'm investigating crimes."

"And you're very concerned about your neighbor."

"I'd be concerned about anyone in a case like this."

"Uh-huh. Right. Any chance you're thinking about that little escapade I walked in on the other night? The one you tried so hard to explain away?"

Ray felt his face heat. "I told you, it was nothing. We're friends."

Philip laughed. "Wish I had more friends like her."

"We *are* friends," Ray protested.

"Okay, and so?" Philip took a swig of coffee. "You can be friends and fall in love. Kissing friends. All the better, I would think."

"No. You don't understand. It can't be that way."

Philip shook his head. "You are stupid. Really, really stupid." His cell phone rang on his belt. He looked at the number and grabbed it. "Yo, Reed here."

His eyes lit up. He stood and punched the OFF button. "That guy came out of his coma."

Ray's mind went on full alert. "You mean the gas station attendant?"

"Yep. C'mon, let's go."

&

Faith opened her front door and tossed her purse on the sofa, expecting the little terrier to come running from the bedroom like she always did. "Sparkles, where are you, girl?" Apprehension tickled her spine. Her cell phone rang in her purse, but she ignored it and walked down the hall to her bedroom. Sparkles's bed was empty.

"Sparkles?" Faith hurried back up the hall to the spare room.

No dog. Almost running now, she hurried to the kitchen. "Sparkles!" The back door to the porch was open. She peered into the screened-in porch. The door to the outside was open, too. Sparkles was gone. Again.

Back in the kitchen, she bit her nails and glanced at the clock on the wall. Peter would be here in a little over an hour. Once again, she wouldn't have the dog. "Calm down," Faith whispered. Ray would be here. He was scheduled to arrive thirty minutes before Peter. She didn't want the time alone with Ray, but she wanted to be alone with Peter even less. Meantime, she'd look for Sparkles outside.

Her cell phone beeped, indicating the person who'd called had left a message. She hurried to the living room and dug her phone from her purse. *Missed call.* She pushed a button, and the screen indicated the call had come from Ray.

She dialed her voice mail to retrieve the message while she opened the front door to go outside, and she slammed into Sparkles's supposed owner.

"Whoa, lady," Peter said, taking a few steps backward from the force of her hit.

"Sorry." Faith looked up into his hard face. "You're early." Had her heart stopped beating? She couldn't breathe.

"Yeah, I got off work early. I've waited long enough to get my dog back."

Like last time, he didn't refer to the dog by name or sex. Faith took a step backward and fumbled for the knob to shut the door. She'd be safer on the front porch.

"What's wrong with you?" Peter frowned down at her. "You lost your voice?" He glanced over her head and scanned the room. "Where's my dog?"

Faith cleared her throat. Time for damage control. "Well. . . she's not here right now."

"What?" He took a step toward her. "I came here for nothing?"

"Well. . .a friend of mine has her. He's bringing her in a minute." Breathing a prayer to God to ask forgiveness for lying, she continued. "You *are* early."

"I can't believe it. You let someone else take my dog?" Peter's face reddened. "For a vet, you're awfully irresponsible."

Faith glimpsed movement from the side of her eye and turned. The young girl was peering through the bushes.

Peter followed her glance. He narrowed his eyes and swore. "That kid!" he hollered as he ran down her porch stairs. "Probably took the dog."

The little girl took off running.

"No!" Faith hurried down the porch stairs to follow Peter. "Leave her alone!"

Her view of Peter disappeared behind trees and hedges on neighboring properties. As much as she hoped Peter wouldn't catch the kid, she knew she was no match for the man. She needed help. She hurried back into her house, locked the door, and dialed Ray. While the phone rang, she heard footsteps on her front porch. Then bangs on the door. "Hey, lady! Let me in."

Peter was back—and he was fuming.

"I'm calling the cops," Faith yelled. She got Ray's voice mail and left a hurried message.

The pounding stopped suddenly, and the footsteps retreated. She heard the roar of an engine and ran to the window. He was leaving. She had just enough time to note his license number. Then her cell phone rang.

twenty-two

"Faith?" Ray said into his phone. He was speeding toward her house as they talked. "Did you get my message?"

"No, I didn't get a chance. But Peter was here. He came early."

"Was there?" he shouted, grasping the steering wheel tighter and feeling sick.

"Yes, was," Faith shouted back. "You're going to break my eardrum if you yell any louder. He was here, but he's gone. It was pretty scary. I was about to call 911."

"Sorry." Ray loosened his hold on the steering wheel. "Is your door locked?"

"Yes. It's locked."

"Good. Stay inside," he ordered. "Now tell me everything that happened."

"Why? What's going on? You're scaring me."

"Just tell me what happened, and then I'll explain."

After he'd listened to what she had to say, he swallowed. She could have been hurt or even killed, and he wouldn't have been there to help. "You sure your door is locked?"

"Yes. Now please tell me why you're so frantic."

He arrived at her house and swerved into her driveway, wheels spitting gravel. "I'm here. As soon as I'm inside, I'll tell you everything."

She was waiting at the front door.

"I thought I told you to lock the door," he growled as he stalked past her.

"I did," she snapped. "But I unlocked it when you arrived." She glared at him. "I'm not a child."

He faced her and sighed. "I know. I'm sorry. I was scared. You could have been hurt."

She relaxed a bit. "I was scared, too."

He wanted to yank her into his arms, hold her tight, and promise to protect her always, but the memory of the kiss was too fresh. Besides, they needed to talk.

"Can we sit?" he asked. He tried not to look into her beautiful brown eyes. He didn't want to be tempted again.

"Spill it," she said.

"Remember that gas station robbery Philip was talking about last night?"

Faith licked her lips and nodded.

"The gas station attendant came out of his coma today. Peter was the man who had robbed the gas station, only that's not his real name."

"I didn't think so," Faith said. "Liar. I hate being lied to." She felt her anger growing.

"The gas station attendant identified a mug shot of Peter. That is his first name, but Davis isn't his last name." Ray smiled grimly. "It gets more serious. A kid with a dog witnessed the robbery."

Faith put her hand to her heart. "Oh no. Maybe Sparkles and the little girl? Remember, Peter chased the kid." Faith pulled a slip of paper from her jeans pocket. "I got his license number."

"Good. Give that to me. I'll call it in, then I'll tell you more."

He called dispatch with the information, and when he was done, he pulled out his notebook. "I need information from you."

Faith nodded. "To think a guy like that was in my home. No wonder he made my skin crawl." She brushed her hands over her bare arms, and he felt another strong pull to hold her.

"So you think it's our kid?" she asked. "The one wandering the neighborhood?"

"Not sure."

Faith gave him a rundown of the events. As he took notes, he could feel the unanswered questions hanging between them. The kiss. Why did it happen? He forced the thought from his mind.

"So what can you tell me?" she asked. "Why was he looking for the dog? That makes no sense."

Ray stood, putting physical distance between them, and dropped his gaze to the notebook in his hand. "There was a kid in the gas station when everything went down. A girl with a dog and a cell phone." He tapped the paper.

Faith breathed. Their eyes locked, and he saw her thoughts click into focus. "You're still thinking it's the kid we've been chasing around the neighborhood, aren't you?"

He nodded. "That's what Philip and I suspect. We also think Peter wanted to use the dog as bait to lure the girl out of hiding." He studied her for a moment, then went to the door. "I have to go back to work. I want you to stay safe. Lock all your doors and keep your cell phone with you." He backed toward the front door. "I'll call Cora and Mabel on my way out to tell them what's happened. They need to keep their doors locked, too."

"Okay." Faith took a step back, and he felt the wall go up. "I'll probably join them. We'll lock ourselves up together."

He was reluctant to leave. "Listen, Faith, we need to talk."

The look in her eyes, her stance, told him her walls got higher.

"Haven't we been talking?"

"Yes, but I mean about the other night. It's sort of—"

"Awkward?"

"Yes, it is that."

She was blinking hard. Was she about to cry? "I'm sorry I upset you."

She shrugged. "Maybe some things are better left unsaid."

"Is that the way you feel?"

"Maybe. I don't know."

"Okay, I'll see you later then. And we'll see." He turned before he walked out. "Remember to lock your door."

He went to his car with a heavy heart. He never meant to

hurt Faith. She was his best friend, when they were teens and now. Ray stood beside his car and called dispatch to ask where he was needed. While he waited, he glanced at Faith's house, reluctant to drive away and leave her alone.

At the sound of a vehicle coming down the street, he turned. Had Peter returned? He waited until the car came into sight. It was Bailey. She pulled alongside his car and opened her window. "I've got to talk to you."

"Now? I'm on duty. We've got a crisis."

His words didn't dissuade her. She got out of her car and smiled.

"This is going to have to wait, Bailey. I've got to—"

"This will take less than a minute. I promise." Bailey pulled in a breath like she was summoning courage. "Ray, I love you." She grasped his arm. "But I feel like you're avoiding me. I've got a surprise planned for you tonight."

"Tonight?" Why was she making plans without consulting him?

"Yes." The smile on her face died as if he'd slapped her. "You don't look happy. I guess—I guess the real question is, can we make this right?"

Truth hit like a wake-up slap to his face. If they were truly a couple, her making plans wouldn't annoy him. He was confused about a lot of things—his calling to the ministry, his occupation, kissing Faith, but this was for sure. "You're forcing me to talk on the run. But if you need an answer right now, I have to say I'm sorry, but it's over." The second he spoke the words, he felt at peace.

Bailey released her grip on her forearm. Her face changed from repentant to callous. "I sort of knew it was too late. I just wish you would've been man enough to tell me right away."

Her anger stemmed from hurt, but he couldn't help that. "I was sincere about trying again. But what happened is too much to overcome." He opened his car door.

Her eyes darted toward Faith's house. "It's *her*, isn't it? Something else you should've told me."

"Her? Faith?" Ray examined the feelings stirring in his heart and shrugged. "Faith and I have been friends since we were kids. We've got a history together, but it's not like that. And I know she doesn't feel that way about me." He remembered the kiss and suddenly wished she did.

"Then you're blind." Bailey took a step back. "Well, I'm not about to crawl, so I guess this is good-bye."

Ray nodded. "I wish you the best, Bailey. I truly do."

Her eyes filled. "Do I get a good-bye hug?" She didn't wait for his response, but stepped up to him and slipped her arms around his chest.

Ray patted her back, but tried to politely step out of her lingering embrace. His radio crackled. Philip was requesting his help. "Listen, I've got to go."

Bailey pulled away, a shaky smile masking her tears. "Take care, Ray. I wish the best for you, too." She ran to her car without a backward glance.

Ray sat behind the wheel with one thought in his head. Bailey said he was blind. Did she see something in Faith's feelings for him that he'd missed? He glanced at Faith's house before pulling away from the curb. With surprise and a sudden lightness of heart, he found himself praying that was true.

twenty-three

Faith paced her living room, a mix of feelings swirling inside her heart. Confusion, worry, fear, hope, anger—it ran the gamut. She stumbled over a dog toy. Did the little girl have Sparkles? Ray had been very concerned.

Faith stood in front of her window and couldn't resist pulling aside the curtain to look out and see if Ray had driven away yet.

He hadn't. Faith blinked and leaned so far forward that her nose pressed against the glass. Was that Bailey? Hugging Ray? In broad daylight, in front of the whole world? Where had she come from? Faith clenched her fists and ordered her feet to stay put, otherwise she'd run from the house screaming and rip Bailey from Ray's arms.

After a torturous moment, she let the curtain drop. *Voyeur!* she chided herself as she stomped to the kitchen, wishing it were morning and she could go to work. How she loved the distraction of the busy clinic. But she should have the right to look out her own window and not have to watch scenes like that! She took a deep breath and unclenched her fists, forcing her body to relax. "I'm sorry, Lord. It's my temper again."

She opened the refrigerator door, then shut it again. She couldn't rid her mind of the picture of Bailey and Ray.

I love him. The thought kept returning, each time with more certainty—and trepidation. When had she fallen in love with Ray? As a teenager? Probably. Back then it was young love, but love nonetheless. And like Debbie said, she was scared of failure, so she let him go rather than take a chance. But through the years he had always been the standard by which she had judged other men, even in the Navy. That was probably why she'd never fallen in love with anyone else.

Faith shook her head. Ray wasn't available. She'd seen it with her very own eyes two minutes ago. He had a thing for Bailey Cummings, despite the fact that she'd cheated on him. And Bailey definitely had a thing for him. Maybe Ray's kiss in the kitchen of the Victorian had been a sort of payback for Bailey's indiscretion.

"I kissed him back," she said with a mocking laugh.

She'd always been Faith the control freak. Faith the woman who kept everything in order, even as a child. As an adult, she realized the habit was more than a personality quirk. She did it so she could keep her emotions orderly. If they weren't orderly, she fell apart, like she had in the office that morning. And all in an effort not to let anything break through the walls she'd built around herself. Now Ray was back, and he had managed to hammer through those walls. She'd let him in, despite her best efforts—a man who was in love with another woman.

She needed to get ahold of herself. She grabbed her sweater and marched to the front door. She'd go see Mabel and Cora. The sisters were supposed to be working on the new place. Just being around them calmed her. Besides, there was safety in numbers.

Faith locked her door, then hurried across the street. There were cars parked along the curb, but none looked like Peter's. She entered the Victorian using a key the sisters had given her and heard noise in the back of the house.

"Cora? Mabel?" She rushed down the hall to the kitchen, all the while calling their names. "There you are!" Faith said.

Mabel held a sponge against the old wallpaper. "Land sakes, child, what a commotion." She dropped the sponge into a bucket and descended the ladder. "You worried about that criminal?"

"Not now. I guess Ray called you?"

"Yessiree. Told me all about it. Said you were safe, praise the Lord for His protection." Mabel pointed at a chair in the middle of the kitchen. "Sit down. You look pale."

Faith complied, but couldn't keep her hands still. She kept tapping her fingers on her thighs.

"I hate to say this, but you're a mess looking for a place to happen. You look like you're going to pop." Mabel moved the bucket aside, wiped her hands on her work apron, then put them on her hips. "Do you need to eat? Cora will be here shortly. She says she has something important to tell me."

"Not hungry, but I could go for some coffee."

"That's the last thing you need. Your hair is already standing on end." Mabel studied her with narrowed eyes.

Faith shook her head. "I'm sorry to bother you. I'm probably not fit for human company today."

"Hush now," Mabel warned. "You know better. You never bother me."

Faith bit at her nails. The image of Ray's eyes when he bent down to kiss her was superimposed in her mind with the image of him and Bailey hugging.

Mabel pulled up a chair next to her. "Now talk to me."

Faith bit her lip, reluctant to blurt the whole truth; but isn't that why she'd come here? And where did she start? With something safe, she decided. "I'm worried about Sparkles and the little girl."

"So are we. We prayed, and we're believing God is in control. He's doing a good work."

"Maybe for some people." As soon as the words were out of her mouth, she knew she sounded like a child. Her problems were nothing compared to the young girl running around the neighborhood alone.

They heard the front door open.

"That would be Cora," Mabel said. "I recognize her footsteps."

"I brought weapons," Cora said as she walked into the kitchen and put a sack on the counter.

"What?" Faith asked.

The plastic rattled as Cora removed a can from the sack. "We're gonna be ready for him if he comes. Why do you think the good Lord made wasp spray?"

Faith laughed. "What would I do without you two?"

"I have some news for you," Cora said as she removed duct tape, trash bags, sponges, and several containers of cleaning products from the sack.

"What are you planning to do?" Faith pointed at the supplies.

"Clean," Cora said, then she waved the duct tape. "And fix a couple of loose things around here until Ray can do it right. Duct tape is good for lots of things." She grinned and put it back in the bag. Then she wiped her hands and turned to Faith and Mabel. "My news can wait for a minute. Looks like this is a serious discussion."

Mabel nodded. "Faith is troubled, but she hasn't told me why yet."

Cora crossed the room and laid her hand on Faith's head. "Lord bless you, child. Talk."

Faith swallowed hard, trying to find a way to open a discussion about her feelings for Ray and what she'd just witnessed from her window. "I, um, just saw Ray."

"Huh-uh." Mabel laughed. "Is that all that's stuck in your head after you were almost accosted by a robber? Ray told us all about it."

" 'Course it is," Cora said, smiling. "Our boy is good-lookin' and charming. A real catch, I say."

"I'd be smiling with you if I hadn't seen Ray and Bailey from my window. . .hugging." Faith searched their faces for a reaction. Nothing. "They were hugging for a really long time," she added, feeling a new wave of anger.

Mabel and Cora exchanged glances, then Cora held up her hand. "Now let's not jump to any conclusions, right, sis?"

Mabel tilted her chin. "I don't blame Faith. I don't like that huggin' stuff either." She tapped Faith's hand. "You ought to have come out of the house with a broom and shooshed that girl away."

As heavy as her heart felt, Faith laughed with the two. "Believe me, I wanted to do worse, but I—"

"If you did that, Ray would know you loved him." Cora looked thoroughly satisfied with her conclusion.

"I...well..." Faith still couldn't say the words out loud.

"Bless your heart," Cora said. "It's like faith. Like accepting Jesus. You just got to screw up your courage and say it out loud."

As usual, the sisters saw right through her. Faith blew out a breath, ready to confess all. "Yes, all right. I'll admit I'm in love with Ray. But what's the point? He's after Bailey, and she's after him. Nobody hugs that long if—"

"He don't look at Bailey like he does you." Mabel's smile got wider. "And Bailey don't look at Ray the way you do."

"Then why the dating? Why the hug?" The sisters were usually right, but maybe they wished so hard for her and Ray to get together that they were blindsided this time.

"What's that poet say?" Cora appeared thoughtful for a moment. " 'Better to have loved and lost than not to have loved at all.' "

"Now that's a fine howdy do." Mabel slapped Cora's arm. "We're trying to encourage Faith. Besides, you should talk, Cora Mae." Mabel rolled her eyes. "You with your beau of a hundred years, Dr. Douglas."

"You don't know nothin'." Cora turned to Faith and winked. "Now honey, you lovin' Ray despite what you see with your eyes, that makes you human instead of a machine who won't let herself feel nothing."

"That's right," Mabel agreed. "It's time you become normal. We been prayin' about that, too. You need to forgive your daddy for being a dumb man. And don't you think we won't investigate that huggin' stuff that went on today. We'll nail that boy to the wall. Bad enough he thought to give that Bailey a second chance. We prayin' for her, don't you think we're not. And we don't wish evil for her, but she's not the one for Ray. No sirree. It would never work."

Cora clapped, sending a shot of adrenaline through Faith. "Lord, show Ray the truth." She grabbed her sister's hand

and Faith's in a spontaneous act of prayer. "Arrest that boy's heart right now, Father, and tell him what You've told us, that they belong together. We pray this in Jesus' name, amen."

Faith nodded her agreement and found herself smiling. She loved these sisters with all her heart and deep inside believed everything would be all right, though she couldn't fathom how that would happen.

"One more thing," Faith said. "I—I kissed Ray."

Both sisters' faces lit with hundred-watt smiles.

She frowned. "I don't think you heard me right. I said we kissed. Right here. In this kitchen."

Cora sniffled and dabbed her eyes with her fingertips. "Now isn't it just like God to make it happen in our new house. A sign of more good to come."

"Amen." Nodding, Mabel stood and pointed at Cora. "Now sis, tell us your good news."

Cora beamed. "You know how I found the grandson of the man who built this house?" She clasped her hands. "He told me a secret. C'mon." She motioned to the basement door. "I'll show you. It's a surprise."

Faith followed the sisters down the sturdy wooden stairs. A rock-walled basement room spread out before them. It smelled dusty, but not damp. Cobwebs hung from the large beams on the ceiling. "Are there other rooms?"

"Don't you know it." Cora's beam grew.

"We gotta clean this up," Mabel said, poking at a low-hanging cobweb.

"Come on!" Cora led them through a wooden door to a room on the right. A couple of windows stood at the top of the walls.

Faith heard a dog whine. Sparkles?

Cora stopped.

"I'm hearing things," Faith said.

"If you are, I am, too," Mabel whispered. "I heard that doggy."

Cora walked to a set of shelves that ran from floor to ceiling and pulled on them. Like a door, they opened, and behind them was a cavity lined with rock that extended beyond the house.

And crouched on the floor against the back was a little girl. A cell phone lay at her feet. She was curled up, crying, holding Sparkles to her chest.

twenty-four

Ray and Philip stood in the small house not far from Mabel and Cora's. Mrs. Wilson, the little girl's grandmother, cried silent tears, clasping and unclasping her hands. "I should have known Sasha was missing, but I thought she was with her mother."

Ray couldn't help but agree with her. She *should* have known the girl was missing, although perhaps he was being too judgmental. He just couldn't stand the thought of kids in danger.

"You haven't called your daughter?"

"Daughter-in-law. Actually, ex-daughter-in-law." Mrs. Wilson looked so pale, he thought she might faint.

"Perhaps you should sit down," he said.

"No! How can you expect me to sit when my Sasha is in danger?" She inhaled. "Has anyone seen Lucky?"

"Who's Lucky?" Philip asked.

"Her dog. They are inseparable."

"A little terrier?" Philip asked.

She nodded, looking at them with a spark of hope.

"The dog has been seen," Ray said.

"But you don't know where Sasha is." The older woman paced across her sparsely furnished living room, tears still falling down her cheeks. An old television flashed commercials in the background. She turned to Philip and Ray. "This is my fault, you know. I got Sasha that cell phone for her birthday. She was twelve. It was all she wanted. I worked extra hours to get her what she wanted. It took pictures—imagine a phone taking a picture. If I hadn't gotten her that phone maybe this wouldn't have happened." She stopped pacing, lowered her head, and sobbed.

Ray and Philip exchanged glances. They had to get her back on track.

"Ma'am, we're sorry, but we have to get more information from you." Philip pointed to the threadbare sofa. "Why don't you have a seat? Can one of us get you something? A glass of water?"

She shook her head and dropped onto the sofa. "No, nothing. I just want my granddaughter back."

"Can you tell us what happened the day she disappeared?" Ray still wondered why the woman hadn't reported Sasha missing.

Mrs. Wilson nodded. "She said she was going for a walk with Lucky, to take some pictures, and then go to her mama's. Her mama lives two blocks away. She's got custody, you know. Next thing I know, Sasha calls and says she's at her mom's and is going to stay there for a while."

"You didn't call her mother?" Ray tried to keep the cynical tone from his voice when what he really wanted to do was ream her out.

" 'Course I did." Mrs. Wilson shook her head. "Her mama wouldn't answer. She refuses to talk to me. That's one reason I got Sasha the phone. So she could call me. But she hasn't answered her phone. I've been so worried. Her mama. . .she's bad news. Her and them people she brings in." She began to cry again. Ray cleared his throat, and Mrs. Wilson continued. "When Sasha's daddy, my son, died, I went to court and tried to get custody. I lost. She could make things bad for me. . . . She's got this boyfriend. . . ."

She kept rubbing her worn hands, her eyes filled with fear. Ray and Philip exchanged glances.

"We need a picture of Sasha," Philip said.

Mrs. Wilson stood and went to an old spinet piano where a series of pictures showed the growth of a girl who was obviously Sasha. "Here's the latest." Her hand trembled as she held the framed photo out to Philip.

"We'll bring it back," he said, indicating the photo, then

he nodded at Ray.

Ray pulled a sketch of Peter from his pocket. "This is the man involved in the robbery. Do you recognize him?"

She took the paper from Ray and frowned at it. "Yes." She inhaled and her face hardened. "That's him! My daughter-in-law's boyfriend. He sometimes lives with Sasha's mother. Stays for days at a time." She gave them the address, and Philip called it in.

"Is he involved?" she asked.

Ray hesitated, and Philip nodded. "We believe so."

"Do you think Sasha is okay?" Mrs. Wilson looked up at Ray, fear etching her face with deep lines. "Will my baby be okay?"

"We hope so," Ray said. He hated this part of his job. Watching people suffer and not being able to help them the way he wanted to because of rules. He had to be politically correct. But as the woman wrung her hands, he crossed the room and put his hand on her shoulder. "Do you go to church, ma'am?"

She blinked. "Yes, I do."

The mic on Philip's shoulder crackled to life, and he excused himself.

"Do you believe in prayer?"

"Yes, I do." The hope in her eyes grew.

"Just know that people are praying for Sasha. I know that for a fact. Let me pray for you and Sasha now."

When they were done, she cried again, but this time with hope. She grasped his hand. "Thank you, officer. You don't know how much that means to me."

Ray felt as if he'd been hit with lightning. *I'm in the wrong career. Now I know. It's like Faith said—that when it happens. . . it's a defining God moment.*

But before he could follow the thought, Philip burst back into the room. "They found the guy's car at Sasha's mother's house. They're interviewing the mother now, but she. . ." Philip paused, and Ray knew he wasn't telling him everything in front of Sasha's grandmother. "Peter took her car, and he's gone."

"He hurt her, didn't he?" Mrs. Wilson said. "He did that a lot."

"I'm sorry, ma'am, we need to go," Philip said.

Ray took Mrs. Wilson's hand. "You just keep praying."

⌘

Along with Mabel and Cora, Faith coaxed the frightened girl upstairs to the kitchen.

"What's your name, baby doll?" Cora asked the girl.

"Sasha," she whispered, clutching at Sparkles so hard the dog yelped.

Faith pulled out her cell phone to call Ray. Mabel shook her head violently and pulled Faith into the hallway.

"That child is scared to death. Let us settle her down before we call in the police. They'll just come roaring in here, lights going, and they'll bring Social Services or something. Poor little tot needs to be prepared for all that commotion." Mabel turned as though the matter were settled.

Faith thought the word "tot" didn't apply. The girl looked to be almost twelve, but she wasn't going to argue the point. "I'm worried. I think Ray needs to know."

Mabel turned back to her. "We won't wait long to call him. Just enough to get some food into her and settle her down."

"Mabel?" Cora called from the kitchen. "The electricity is on now. I'm going across the street to get that pot of chicken soup from the refrigerator. And biscuits. I'll need your help. And we're safe together."

"Right!" Mabel said from the hallway. She pushed Faith back into the kitchen. "You keep that child company. You can talk to her about the dog. She'll like that. You two got a lot in common. We'll get food and be right back. And don't worry, we'll call Ray, too."

The sisters bustled from the house, and Faith was left alone with Sasha, whose wide eyes left no doubt she was just as stunned as Faith by the whirlwinds called Cora and

Mabel.

Faith reached down and stroked Sparkles's head.

"You took good care of Lucky, didn't you?" Sasha looked up with a watery gaze.

"Lucky? Is that her name?"

Sasha nodded, and a smile broke through.

Faith pulled a chair up and sat next to the girl, but Sasha drew back as though afraid of being touched. She recognized something in the child that she saw in herself. Walls. *Don't let anyone too close. You might get hurt.*

Faith scooted her chair back to give Sasha space. "Lucky is a good dog."

"I know." She hugged the dog. "I was so scared that day. I was running away from Peter." She inhaled. "My mama doesn't live far from here, but I couldn't stay with her. Peter would find me. Anyway, Lucky got away from me, and I had to chase her." Sasha watched Faith warily, her blue eyes wide.

Faith reached out to brush the girl's bangs out of her eyes, but pulled back her hand. She needed to make Sasha feel safe first. "You've been taking food from people's houses, now haven't you?"

Sasha nodded, and fresh tears filled her eyes.

"How did you get into this house? And how did you know about the secret room?"

"A lady down the street. She let me stay in her shed until her husband found out. She told me where to hide so no one could find me, and I crawled in the basement window. But you did find me."

"Yes, we did."

"I'm going to jail, I know I am," she whispered. "If I don't die."

"If you don't die? Why would you die?"

"Peter said he'd kill me and Granny and Lucky if I told anybody about what he did."

Faith's heart lurched. "When did he say that to you?"

"After he robbed the gas station. I tried to run away, but he grabbed my shirt and said that. Then I kicked him hard and ran." Sasha twisted her small hands in her lap, and her chest rose and fell as though she could see Peter.

"Oh, sweetheart." Faith swallowed around the lump in her throat.

"I saw him in his car watching my granny's house, so I couldn't go back there. I wanted to. And I wanted to call Granny, but my phone battery died. I didn't know what to do. . . ." Her voice broke.

Anger like fire hit Faith that the poor child had been threatened by Peter. "Don't worry. My friend Ray will take care of Peter." *I'd like to take him on myself for what he's done.* She took a breath, willing her anger to simmer. "Can you tell me what happened? How did Lucky get hurt?"

Sasha nodded. "I got this glittery card and a new cell phone for my birthday, and I went to take pictures."

"I love taking pictures," Faith said, trying to bring levity to the situation. "It's my hobby. And your grandma allowed you to go to the gas station alone?"

Sasha raised her chin. "I'm twelve."

"I know," Faith said. She didn't want to judge, but in this day and age—

Sasha sucked in her lower lip. "The gas station is at our corner. Lucky started pulling me in that direction. I got money for my birthday, too, so I wanted to buy candy."

"I see." Faith brushed her hand over Sasha's hair, and this time the girl didn't shy away.

"Peter. . .he's a drug dealer. I knew that because sometimes he did it at my mom's house."

Faith's heart broke for this young girl who had seen too much. A sudden flash of insight hit her like a slap. Her life hadn't been as bad as she'd allowed herself to believe. In fact, she was blessed. Mabel was right. She needed to forgive her father. He might have been strict, too strict, and distant—not nearly as loving as he could have been—but Faith had never had to deal with the horror Sasha had been through.

"I was already in the store when Peter walked in. When he started robbing the gas station man, I hid behind where the potato chips are and took pictures of him. But Lucky started barking, and Peter saw me." Sasha's lip trembled again. "He kicked Lucky, and he grabbed my shirt. He said, 'Give me that phone.' But I kicked him and got away. I kept on running. . . .'"

"That was smart, Sasha." Faith brushed a tear off her cheek, and a new thought struck. "You took Lucky both times before Peter came to my house to get her. How did you know he was coming for Lucky?"

"I was hiding in my mom's house and heard Peter say it." Sasha lowered her gaze. "And. . .the other time I heard you talkin' on the phone. . ." Fresh tears filled the girl's eyes.

Faith held her close. "It's going to be all right, Sasha. Do you believe me?"

The sound of the front door opening behind her sent relief through Faith. Footsteps came down the hall. "Ray?"

Sasha let loose a blood-curdling screech.

Faith turned. "Oh no. . ." She leaped to her feet and grabbed Sasha to run.

"Don't move," Peter said, brandishing a pistol. "It's my lucky day. I can take care of my problems all at once."

twenty-five

Lucky barked frantically, wiggling in Sasha's arms.

"How did you know I...we...were here?" Faith drew Sasha closer.

"Been parked down the street. Knew those two old women left. You were here alone, I thought. But now...I've got what I was looking for." He pointed the gun at Sasha. "It's time to come home."

Lucky growled and leaped from Sasha's arms.

"No!" the girl screamed.

Faith tried to grab the little dog, but she ran past them, right for Peter's legs. Without taking his eyes off Faith, Peter gave the animal a swift kick. Lucky yelped, then limped under the table and collapsed.

Sasha was sobbing now, hanging onto Faith.

"The police are on their way," Faith threatened, taking another step back.

"No way. Not yet. They're busy with Sasha's mom. After I got done with her, she's not gonna talk."

Faith saw motion over his shoulder. Cora and Mabel appeared in the doorway. Mabel had her finger to her lips. Faith's heart sped faster. Sasha's wails and the dog's yapping must have covered the noise of them coming into the house. Faith kept her face rigid. The sisters would know what to do—as long as Peter didn't hear them.

Faith had to keep talking. "You won't get away with this. The police will find you and you'll pay."

"Shut up," he spat.

Faith fought for deeper breaths. She had to do something to keep Peter from hearing the sisters and so pretended to break down in sobs.

Mabel held a basket in one hand. Cora walked into the kitchen, balancing a pot in her hands.

"What are you going to do with us?" Faith wailed louder.

Cora lifted the pot above her head.

"I ask the questions," Peter said. "Now shut your mouth and stop that infernal noise."

Cora lifted her arms higher and then dropped the pot on Peter's head. Chicken soup sloshed everywhere, and the pot and lid hit his shoulders and clanged to the floor.

Peter staggered and lunged for Faith, but he slipped on the soup and fell flat on his face.

"Shame on you!" Mabel yelled. "You're lucky that soup wasn't boiling, you hoodlum!" She dumped the contents of the basket on Peter, and biscuits bounced over his head and onto the floor.

"For once, I wish your biscuits weren't so fluffy," she said to Cora.

Peter struggled to stand again, but Mabel knocked him over with a single shove.

"Glory to God!" Cora yelled and sat down hard on the small of his back. "This'll teach you, young man. You hear me? Ain't nobody gonna hurt our kin."

"Vengeance is mine, sayeth the Lord!" Mabel pointed at him. "Trying to hurt a child. Hurting her mother. And kicking a dog. Not to mention *thinking* about hurting Faith. You are a bad man!"

Peter struggled under her. "I—can't—breathe."

"That's the least of your worries," Cora said. "Officer Ray Reed is on his way. You'll be answering to the law soon." She planted herself harder on his back. He gave up with a moan. "Sister," Cora pointed at the bag on the counter. "Get the duct tape."

Mabel did so and fastened his feet first, then, without too much of a struggle, she taped his hands together. "Like Cora said, this stuff is good for nearly everything."

Silence reigned for nearly a minute. Faith gazed at the

scene. Noodles, bits of celery, onion, carrot, and pieces of chicken littered the kitchen floor. The pot was lying on its side. Biscuits were strewn from one end of the room to the other. Mabel and Cora were like rescuing angels. Even Sasha had stopped crying, although she wouldn't have been able to continue with her mouth gaping open like it was.

Mabel looked down and pointed at Peter. "'The Lord's curse is on the house of the wicked, but he blesses the home of the righteous.' Proverbs chapter three, verse thirty-three."

"Preach it, sister!" Cora bounced on Peter's back with more exuberance.

Sasha started to giggle. "I've heard of people being *socked*, but not *souped*."

Faith high-fived the girl. Mabel grinned. Cora snorted. Then they all began to laugh.

As Faith wondered what they were going to do with the "souped" bad guy, she heard the front door bang open over the laughter and Ray call her name.

"That boy never did learn how to come into a house quietly." Mabel clucked her tongue.

Cora shook her head. "Gets hisself all worked up and then dents the wall with the doorknob."

Faith wiped tears from her eyes. "In the kitchen, Ray," she said between gasps of laughter.

"Faith! Are you okay?" His question was followed by the sound of several people storming down the hallway. Ray skidded into the kitchen and stopped. Philip slammed into his back. Their wide gazes took in the scene.

"What—what. . .happened here?" Ray asked.

Philip walked around Ray and into the kitchen. "For crying out loud! This is the most amazing thing I've ever seen."

"Calm down and arrest him!" Mabel ordered, pointing at Peter.

"Let me up," Peter groaned.

"How did you. . .never mind." Ray took cuffs from his belt and started for Peter, walking gingerly on the messy floor.

"You won't need them things." Cora pointed at the handcuffs.

Peter wiggled. "Get me away from these crazy women. You're the police, help me!"

"You hush, young man." Mabel pointed at Peter's hands. "Nope, you won't need those, Ray. He's trussed better than a Thanksgiving turkey."

"I can see that," Ray said, exchanging a grin with Philip. He glanced over at Faith. "Are you all right?"

She nodded, feeling suddenly shy.

Ray took a deep breath. "I was so scared—"

He was interrupted by yelling from the front of the house.

"It's all clear," Philip hollered. Thundering footfalls raced down the hall.

"Lord have mercy," Cora said. "Sounds like an army."

"See what I mean by all that cop commotion?" Mabel glared at Faith, but she was having trouble keeping her eyes off Ray.

Several other officers charged into the room and halted, and like Ray and Philip, stared wide-eyed at the suspect on the floor.

"I've never seen anything like this in my life," one of them whispered in awe.

"Perhaps we need to hire you ladies," Philip said.

"Not in this lifetime," Mabel said. "I got other work to do than catch bad guys for the police."

Everyone started laughing, but Faith continued to gaze at Ray. He looked so handsome. *Always the hero,* she mused and felt her emotional walls crumbling and her love for him growing. But was it too late?

"That man made me waste a perfectly good pot of chicken soup," Cora grumbled. "I made it from scratch."

"Well, it's like I always say." Mabel planted her hands on her hips. "Chicken soup is good for whatever ails you."

twenty-six

The next afternoon Ray walked into the Cape Cod, and the sisters were waiting for him in the living room, their arms crossed over their midsections.

"I just got off work and went over to see Faith. She's not there." He rubbed his tired eyes and recounted in his mind for what seemed like the hundredth time how near he came to losing her.

"Sit down," Cora demanded, and he caught one of Mabel's dirty looks on the way to the sofa.

"What's wrong? What did I do this time? Is everybody okay?" Ray searched the two frowning faces.

"Oh, everybody's okay," Mabel said, "if we're not counting Faith's feelings."

"Faith's feelings?"

"Hush, young man and sit yourself on the couch." Mabel pointed. "And make sure your gun is turned off in this house."

Ray obeyed, flipping the safety, feeling like he was twelve.

Cora began to pace. "Huggin' up like that." She shook her head side to side. "In broad daylight, with a woman who you aren't in love with."

"What?" Ray scrubbed his hand over his five o'clock shadow. "Did I miss something?"

They both chuckled in that way that told him nothing was funny, then Mabel harrumphed. "In my day you didn't go huggin' up in public for all the neighbors to see. Especially with someone you have no business huggin' up to."

"Like it's something to be proud of," Cora added.

"Huggin' up?" Exhausted, he fought to get their meaning. "I've had a long day helping to wind up this case. Trying to make sure Sasha doesn't get charged for breaking and

162

entering and stealing stuff. . .and. . .I'm so confused. Can we start from the beginning?"

Cora stopped in front of him. "We'll discuss Sasha in a moment, so don't you get all cop-ish with Miss Cora and Miss Mabel. You might have a badge, but you're in our house now, and we're in charge. We have more important fish to fry at the moment. Besides, that child will be just fine."

"Yes indeedy," Mabel said. "We have connections."

"Connections. . . ," he mumbled.

"That means we're taking care of Sasha," Mabel said.

"Now don't change the subject," Cora said. "We were discussing your misbehavior."

Ray shifted on the sofa cushion, wishing he'd stayed at work. "I'm sorry, but I have no idea what you're talking about."

"You'd better not be playing dumb on purpose." Mabel lowered her lids like he wasn't worth a second look. "It's that Bailey, and right outside Faith's house, putting her paws all over you."

"You think we don't know." Cora snorted and looked him in the eye.

"Bailey?" Ray whispered. "Bailey had her paws all over me? When did you see Bailey with her paws, er, hands all over me?"

"Not us. *Faith* saw Bailey," Mabel said. "And you."

"Faith saw Bailey and me—"

"That's what we're sayin'," Cora huffed. "For such a smart boy, you aren't acting it."

"Okay, I give up. I'm clueless today. When did Faith see this?"

"Yesterday," Mabel hissed. "In her driveway."

Light dawned. Ray couldn't help but smile.

"What're you grinning about?" Cora looked over at Mabel, then back at Ray. "You come home to mend a relationship—"

"Aha, I get it now." Faith was mad because she'd seen Bailey hug him. That was very good news. "I was saying good-bye to Bailey—"

"And you have mended fences," Mabel said, "but not the one you thought needed mending."

"It's over with Bailey."

Cora and Mabel both stopped and stared down at him.

"I agree with everything you've both said. Bailey was only hugging me good-bye, and it wasn't my idea." Ray looked from one lovely sister to the other. "I love her. With all my heart."

"You best be talkin' about Faith." Cora gave him a challenging glare.

"I am. I'm talking about Faith. I love her."

"It's about time!" Cora shouted.

"Then what are you doing sittin' here?" Mabel pointed to the front door. "Faith's at the clinic. Get yourself in gear and get over there now."

Ray stood. "Shouldn't I change my clothes first?"

Mabel wagged her head. "Lands sake, Ray, you oughta know better."

"Women love men in uniform," Cora said, and both sisters laughed.

❧

Lucky was bruised, but thankfully she had survived another attack by Peter. Lucky, indeed. Her name should be Blessing. This one little dog had done more to bring people together and help mend relationships than any pet she'd ever met. Faith set her on a cushion in her office and patted her head.

Lucky sighed and stared at the door.

"I know—you want Sasha. Just you wait. Her grandma is bringing her to get you."

Faith shook her head as she sat down at her desk and began to doodle. Mabel and Cora had pulled some strings to help Sasha. Who knew they had those kinds of connections? Not only was no one charging Sasha for stealing and breaking into their homes, but Social Services had given temporary custody to her grandmother until things could be permanent in court.

She looked down at her doodles. All hearts. That told her exactly whom she was trying not to think about. *Ray.* She hadn't seen him since he took Peter away the night before. She'd gone straight home, dropped into bed, and fell into a dreamless sleep. For the first time in months, she slept straight through the night. As though the Lord had healed something inside her—and He had. For the first time in her life, she wasn't afraid to love. She looked down at the heart doodles again. *Ray, I love you.*

She'd have to tell him, even if he couldn't return her feelings. That way she'd be free to move on.

"Dr. Hart?" Gladys peeked her head in the office.

Faith dropped her pen and looked up. "Yes?"

"Your father is on the phone. Says it's important."

Her father. "Okay. I'll take the call."

Gladys hesitated. "Mr. Rees is in examining room one with his three Dobermans."

"Are Thor and Zeus huddled against his legs, shaking? And is Samson retching in the corner?"

Gladys nodded. "And Mrs. MacInnis is in examining room three with her cat. She's got hair balls."

"Mrs. MacInnis has hair balls?" Faith smiled.

After a hesitant chuckle, Gladys shook her head. Faith had a ways to go before her staff wouldn't be nervous around her. "Ask Lindsey if she'll go in and do the initial work. I'll be there in a couple minutes. And thank you."

"Um, you're welcome," Gladys said and shut the door.

Faith stared at the phone and thought about Sasha and once again realized she had much to be grateful for. Though her dad had never been affectionate. . . Faith sighed. Okay, even by normal standards he'd be considered too strict. But he'd always given her everything she needed. Maybe she needed to give him a break. Crack the ice and see what kind of potential lay underneath.

She picked up the phone. "Dad?"

"Faith! I got a call from some person named Mabel. She

said you were involved in a kidnap attempt. What's happening there?"

Faith paused. How did Mabel get her father's phone number? There was a lot she didn't know about the sisters. "Mabel said all that?"

"Yes. And you helped capture a known felon."

"I'm not sure it's quite like that," Faith admitted.

"Well, what happened?" he demanded.

Faith explained, and after a long pause, he groaned. "You could have been killed." It was a statement, not a question. "All for a dog and a little girl." Another statement.

"Sort of, I guess," Faith said, waiting for the criticism.

"I see." His voice was lower than normal.

After thirty seconds she realized he wasn't going to criticize her, and her heart felt lighter. "Dad, I have something to tell you."

"What's that?"

"I've been thinking lately and—and I want you to know that I appreciate everything you've ever done for me."

"Well. I should think so." He harrumphed. "Your brother will be coming into port soon."

For the first time she wondered if this was her father's awkward way of carrying on a conversation. Fact or not, she would take it as such. "Yes, I know. And I will attend the picnic celebrating his return."

"Good," he said. "Richard will like that."

There was a knock on her office door. "Faith? We need you," Debbie called.

"Dad, I have to go. I have clients. Oh—I love you." She didn't give him a chance to respond, just hung up. Let him think about that for a while.

"What is it?" she asked. "Come in."

Debbie cracked the door and poked her head through the opening. "You're wanted out front."

Faith drew a breath and shook her head. "I've got two examining rooms full. Can you deal with it?"

"No, I cannot." Debbie's voice was firm. "You must come out front. Please."

"Who needs me?"

"Faith, do I ever intrude on your day for trivial tasks?"

"No. I'm sorry." Faith stood and straightened her white jacket and followed Debbie to the front.

"What is it?" she whispered.

"Some guy said he has to see you. . .right now. It's urgent."

Faith gave up asking questions. She opened the door to the waiting room area and halted.

"Ray?"

He stood in his uniform, tall and posture ramrod straight. Three other clients sat in chairs watching her with wide eyes. They probably thought he was there to question her.

Ray walked the few steps toward her slowly. "Thank you for coming out here, Dr. Hart."

Faith took a step toward him. Why was he calling her doctor? She glanced at her clients as though they had the answer, but they looked how she felt—worried.

"The other night your actions caused some serious issues."

She took two steps toward him, motioning him with a finger to her lips to keep his voice down. "What are you talking about? Issues with what?"

"You and me. You're going to have to be taken into custody."

"What? What do you mean?" She moved closer until she could smell his aftershave. "Ray, if this is a joke. . . ," she whispered. "You're in uniform. My clients think I've committed a crime."

"You have." Ray placed his hands on her upper arms and pulled her to him. "You've stolen my heart."

The elderly Mrs. Bancroft smiled, then covered her mouth with her hand. The man sitting two seats away from her turned down his mouth and nodded as though he were proud of Ray's boldness. Tracy Como chewed her nail like she was watching a scary movie.

Had Faith heard him right? "What are you saying?"

"You've stolen my heart. So you have to pay a fine. I need yours in return."

"You need my. . .heart?"

Ray looked over his shoulder. "I just told her what I want, didn't I?"

All three of her clients nodded as Ray dropped to one knee in front of her.

"I love you, Faith. If you love me, too, we'll get married and fill our house with lots of babies."

"Married? Babies?"

"Just say yes," Debbie squealed.

"Yes?" Faith heard herself say.

"Say you love him, too," Lindsey said behind her.

"I love you, too." Faith blinked, and the full impact of what was happening finally hit. She reached for his outstretched hands. "I think I've always loved you, Ray Reed."

"Will you marry me?"

Nodding and smiling, she said, "Yes!"

Ray stood, and a single tear ran down his cheek. "You need to know I'm going to be a music minister, not a cop."

"Oh, Ray," she whispered. She wiped his tear with her index finger. "My sensitive musician. That's the perfect job for you."

He cupped her face with his hands and kissed her soundly. When he was done, he backed up and smiled. "I'll bet Mabel and Cora would approve of *that* public display of affection."

"Oh, I have no doubt," she said and threw her arms around his neck.

epilogue

The October sky was never brighter or bluer. After quickly crossing the road from her house, making sure that Ray was nowhere in sight, Faith stood on the steps of the Victorian mansion in jeans and a sweatshirt, her long hair still in rollers. She tapped at the front door before going in, then stood in the large entry hall and visually scanned the room and the staircase. Colorful bunches of flowers were tied to the banisters as far as she could see. Chrysanthemums filled vases everywhere, and a white runner stood beside the french doors off the dining room, waiting to be unfurled.

Faith stood in silence, alone, hand over her heart. Today she would become Faith Anne Reed. She looked down at her sparkly engagement ring. In just a while she would don a matching wedding band.

"I thought I heard the front door open." Mabel came waltzing up to Faith and wrapped her in a tight hug. "Now get upstairs and get dressed. The girls are waiting."

Faith nodded. "Thank you for all this, Miss Mabel. How will I ever repay you and Cora?"

Cora came down the staircase. "You and Ray live a long and happy life together and raise your children in the admonition of the Lord."

"Teach them His ways," Mabel added. "That's repayment enough. Now git!" She pointed up the staircase, and Faith laughed.

Debbie, her matron of honor, greeted her with a squeal. "Look at my makeup." She batted her eyelids. "We've got a real makeup artist."

"You look fabulous," Faith said. "Do I go next?"

She was summoned over by Lori, the cosmetologist, so she

scooted past Debbie and settled in the chair.

"Your bone structure is perfect," Lori said. "You won't need much to make you shine."

"Thanks. I don't wear heavy makeup, so that's good." Faith folded her shaky hands on her lap. In two hours she'd be Mrs. Reed. She closed her eyes and thanked God she would marry her best friend and the man of her dreams.

A knock came at the door, and Debbie went off to open it.

Faith heard the deep rumble of her dad's voice and felt her heart sink. Today she needed his affirmation and approval. "Please, Lord," she whispered.

Debbie stepped back, and her father entered the room with military bearing and an expression she could not decipher.

"Excuse me, Lori." Faith stood, straighter than usual, and approached him. "Hi, Dad, what's wrong?"

He clamped his hands behind his back. "Why does something have to be wrong?" His lips turned up in a smile. "You are beautiful." He reached out awkwardly, gave her a hug, stepped back, and took her hands in his. "Did I ever tell you how proud I am of my daughter?"

Faith laughed through a sudden spate of tears. Her dad almost always spoke of his children in third person.

"Don't cry," Lori and Debbie said almost simultaneously. "Your makeup," Lori added.

Faith sniffled. "I'm not sure you ever told me you're proud of me, Dad." She shrugged. "Or maybe I've forgotten."

He nodded slowly. "Maybe I didn't say it enough. Things were hard after your mother died. But you did turn out fine." Despite his tough words, he was blinking back tears. For the first time in her life, Faith thought he might shed tears. He tilted his chin and cleared his throat. "I'm proud of you, Faith. Now"—he glanced at his watch—"it's twelve hundred hours. I'll leave you to get ready."

When Faith returned to the chair, Debbie was trying to hide tears. "Your makeup," Faith warned with a little laugh. "This is the happiest day of my life," she said with all the conviction in her heart. She again closed her eyes and thanked her heavenly Father.

❧

Ray paced the large kitchen in the Victorian, distracting himself by watching Mabel and Shannon interact. He was thrilled that his good friend from the Tri-Cities was able to attend the wedding with her husband, Glen. And she and Faith had become fast friends.

"Now what's this stuff you're mashin' up?" Mabel asked. Cora stood beside her sister, shaking her head.

Shannon continued to assemble the dish. "It's couscous with broccoli and—" She gasped and put her hand to her stomach. "He's kicking again."

Both sisters smiled broadly. "You know it's a he?" Cora asked.

Shannon's eyes grew wide, and she wagged her head. "Oh no, I'm just guessing. I wouldn't get a sonogram."

"Quite right." Glen looked up from where he sat at the kitchen table, sipping tea. "Shannon says the high-frequency waves disturb the baby's inner peace."

Ray held back a laugh. "Some things never change."

"Indeed," Glen said with a sneaky smile.

"Have you seen the sunroom, Ray?" Shannon asked. "It's amazing beyond words."

Ray shook his head. "No, Miss Mabel and Miss Cora said I'm not allowed in there yet."

"That's right," the sisters said. "You try to sneak a peek again"—Cora grabbed a magazine off the counter and rolled it up—"I'll hit you in the head with this."

"I believe it." Ray laughed long and hard with the other guests, then sobered. "Miss Cora beat me a few times," he announced. "And she'll do it again."

His brother and best man, Philip, poked his head into the kitchen. "She beat me, too."

Ray couldn't resist hanging an arm around each of the sisters' strong shoulders. "That's what all moms do."

Mabel swatted him with a dish towel but couldn't hide the tears in her eyes. "You sure look handsome, son."

"Uh-huh." Cora was nodding and dabbing at her face. "Now where'd your mama go? We're glad she managed to fly back for the wedding."

Ray tilted his head toward the sunroom. "She said she wouldn't have missed it. She's somewhere around here talking to people. You know how she is."

The sisters nodded.

"Okay, everybody." Pastor Gary entered the kitchen, smiling. "It's time. Take your places."

Ray followed his brother into the sunroom. "You should have done this first. You're old, you know."

"Ha!" Philip shook his head. "It'll be a couple of years before I get single life out of my system."

"We'll see." Ray scanned the beautiful room, his heart overflowing with appreciation for all the work Mabel and Cora put into preparing the place. He nodded a greeting to his mom, and she blew him a kiss.

They stood at the altar. How had this all come together so quickly? Ray smiled and answered his own question. *The hand of God is on our lives,* he mused. *Thank You, Lord, for bringing Faith back into my life.*

The music commenced, and the sunroom doors were opened by white-gloved attendants. Ray's breath caught at the sight of his beautiful bride. He suddenly got choked up and came close to tears.

Promising to love and cherish Faith all the days of his life would not be an effort. He had loved and cherished her since he'd been a teen. They'd both taken detours in life, but God brought them right back to Bothell, to their old neighborhood. The Lord worked all things out for the good.

Faith slipped her hand in his, and they faced one another as Pastor Gary had them repeat their vows—the words spoken in the Bible by the Lord Himself.

"The Lord God said, 'It is not good for the man to be

alone.'" Pastor Gary looked into their faces. "And He brought Faith Anne Hart into Ray Reed's life a long, long time ago." He smiled and winked at Ray. "I wondered for a long time when I'd be officiating at their wedding."

"Oh, amen to that!" one of the sisters called out.

After the giggles from the congregation, Ray slipped the wedding band on Faith's slim finger. "I love you so much, Faith."

"I love you more," she whispered.

They kissed to the sound of applause from the wedding guests.

A Letter To Our Readers

Dear Reader:
In order that we might better contribute to your reading enjoyment, we would appreciate your taking a few minutes to respond to the following questions. We welcome your comments and read each form and letter we receive. When completed, please return to the following:

Fiction Editor
Heartsong Presents
PO Box 719
Uhrichsville, Ohio 44683

1. Did you enjoy reading *Mending Fences* by Candice Speare and Nancy Toback?
   ❑ Very much! I would like to see more books by this author!
   ❑ Moderately. I would have enjoyed it more if

   _____

   _____

   _____

2. Are you a member of **Heartsong Presents**? ❑ Yes ❑ No
   If no, where did you purchase this book? _____

   _____

3. How would you rate, on a scale from 1 (poor) to 5 (superior), the cover design? _____

4. On a scale from 1 (poor) to 10 (superior), please rate the following elements.

   ____ Heroine   ____ Plot
   ____ Hero   ____ Inspirational theme
   ____ Setting   ____ Secondary characters

5. These characters were special because? _____

_____

_____

6. How has this book inspired your life? _____

_____

_____

7. What settings would you like to see covered in future
   Heartsong Presents books? _____

_____

_____

8. What are some inspirational themes you would like to see
   treated in future books? _____

_____

_____

9. Would you be interested in reading other **Heartsong
   Presents** titles? ❏ Yes ❏ No

10. Please check your age range:
    ❏ Under 18   ❏ 18-24
    ❏ 25-34   ❏ 35-45
    ❏ 46-55   ❏ Over 55

Name _____

Occupation _____

Address _____

City, State, Zip _____

E-mail _____